P A W N S

Books by Willo Davis Roberts

PAWNS

WILLO

DAVIS

ROBERTS

A JEAN KARL BOOK

ALADDIN PAPERBACKS

New York London Toronto Sydney Singapore

First Aladdin Paperbacks edition April 2000

Copyright © 1998 by Willo Davis Roberts

Aladdin Paperbacks
An imprint of Simon & Schuster Children's Publishing Division
1230 Avenue of the Americas
New York, NY 10020

Book design by Nina Barnett.
Also available in an Atheneum hardcover edition.
The text for this book was set in Granjon.
Printed and bound in the United States of America.
2 4 6 8 10 9 7 5 3

The Library of Congress has cataloged the hardcover edition as follows:
Roberts, Willo Davis.
Pawns / Willo Davis Roberts
p.   cm.
"A Jean Karl book"
Summary: After her mother's death and her father's suicide, fourteen-year-old Teddi finds some stability when she moves in with Mamie, her good-hearted next-door neighbor-until the arrival of a woman claiming to be the pregnant wife of Mamie's son, who recently died in a plane crash.
ISBN 0-689-81668-5 (hc.)
[1. Orphans-Fiction. 2. Death-Fiction. 3. Swindlers and swindling-Fiction. 4. Mystery and detective stories.] I. Title.
PZ7.R5446Pat   1998
[Fic]-dc21   97-36505
ISBN 0-689-83320-2 (pbk.)

PAWNS

Chapter 1

THE DOORBELL RANG.

Teddi put down her book and gave herself a cursory glance in the hall mirror as she passed it. Looking at your own image might be a primary preoccupation for many fourteen-year-olds, but she didn't like her looks all that much. She was too skinny, too pale, and her dishwater-blond hair was no help.

She hesitated, hoping maybe Mamie would show up to answer the summons, but there was no indication that she was even in the house. Probably out in back, weeding the garden, Teddi thought.

She reached for the knob and opened the door.

A girl stood there. Older than Teddi, maybe nineteen or

twenty, at a guess. Rather pretty, in a washed-out way, was Teddi's initial evaluation. Pale brown hair, oddly pale brown eyes as well. The most notable thing about her was that she was in an advanced stage of pregnancy.

The girl smiled a bit uncertainly.

"Yes?" Teddi asked. "We're not interested in buying anything."

The smile became tremulous. "I'm Dora," she said, twisting her hands together over her bulging stomach.

Teddi stared at her blankly. She'd never heard Mamie mention anyone by that name.

"Dora," the girl repeated nervously. And then, realizing that something more was necessary, she added, "Dora, Ricky's wife."

For a few seconds the words did not register. And then, as realization slowly dawned, Teddi drew in a sharp breath.

Ricky's wife?

There was a roaring in her ears, and her vision dimmed momentarily. She held on to the doorknob, bracing against the dizziness that swept over her. Her mouth was so dry, she could barely form the words.

"Ricky's wife?"

Dora's smile wavered. "I don't think I know who you are. Ricky didn't have a sister, did he?"

Teddi swallowed. "No, I'm . . . I lived next door, until my father died. . . . I'm Teddi."

"Oh, and you're visiting Mamie?" Dora didn't wait for a reply, but bent her knees enough to pick up the two suitcases Teddi hadn't noticed until now. "How nice of you. I hope Mamie—Mrs. Thrane—is here?"

She took two steps forward, without being invited, and involuntarily Teddi stepped backward, out of her way. This allowed Dora to enter the house, where her heels clicked on the hardwood floor.

"Teddi, have you seen my . . ."

Behind her, Mamie's voice faltered to a stop upon seeing that they had a visitor. "Oh. Who's this?"

Teddi's vision had cleared, though she still felt she was swallowing cotton.

Even then, she would swear later, she had a premonition of disaster in the making, though she couldn't have explained why. Not exactly.

Teddi tried to speak, but it was Dora who made it first. "Mrs. Thrane? Mamie?"

"Yes," Mamie said, approaching them, peeling off a gardening glove. A tentative smile touched her lips.

"I'm Dora," the girl said, moistening her lips while Teddi remained frozen, unable even to close the front door.

"Dora?" Mamie, too, echoed the name, bewildered.

"Ricky's wife," Dora asserted, allowing her smile to appear again, as if anticipating Mamie's welcome.

For long seconds Mamie stood there, her graying hair slightly mussed, the knees of her faded jeans revealing dirt and moisture, her own smile congealing on her lips. Her gaze swung toward Teddi, evaluating *her* reaction, and then her ungloved hand crept to her throat.

It was a good thing there was a chair beside the hall

table. Mamie sank onto it as the blood drained from her face.

When Mamie, too, was stricken, Teddi threw off her own shock. "I'll get you a glass of water," she offered, and fled past the newcomer toward the kitchen.

Behind her she heard Mamie say, "I'm afraid I don't understand." And then the girl's voice, full of concern: "You mean he didn't tell you about me?"

Mamie's words were tremulous. "I'm afraid I misunderstood you. You couldn't have said you were *Ricky's wife*."

"Oh, dear," Dora said in distress. "I'm so sorry. I was sure he would have told you. . . ."

In the kitchen, Teddi turned on the cold water tap and filled a glass, then hurried back to Mamie with it.

The older woman seemed incapable of lifting a hand to take it, so Teddi held it for her. Mamie took only a few sips.

Dora had put down the suitcases and was again twisting her hands together. Her eyes sought Teddi's.

"I didn't expect to be a horrible surprise to her. Ricky never *told* me he'd written to his mother about me, but I assumed he had. . . ."

Teddi's response came painfully. "Ricky's dead. He died two weeks ago in a plane crash."

Dora bit her lip. "Yes. Only twenty-six years old, and to be snuffed out like that, in an instant. Please, Mamie—may I call you that, or would you prefer that I call you Mother? I don't have a mother of my own, not since I was twelve, and I—" She faltered, then deliberately firmed up her voice. "I was hoping to find a family here. . . ."

Mamie's throat worked before she could speak. "My . . . my other daughter-in-law calls me Mamie," she said.

"Mamie, then." Dora gave them a watery smile. "It's such a sad way to meet, isn't it? Not at all the way I'd imagined. Well, I wonder if I could sit down? I walked the last few blocks from the bus stop, and I get tired pretty fast these days." For a moment her hand rested protectively on her bulging stomach.

Mamie was pulling herself together with an effort. "Yes, of course. Let's go into the living room." She reached out a hand to Teddi, and it was ice-cold as Teddi helped her to her feet.

They made their way into the cozy sitting room, full of old but comfortable furniture. Teddi suddenly saw it through a stranger's eyes. Shabby, it was. A little untidy, with her own book lying on the end of the couch, and today's paper on the floor beside Mamie's chair.

Mamie almost slid into her rocker, and for once she didn't immediately put her feet up onto the stool. It was as if the effort was too much for her.

Dora had brought her luggage with her, putting both cases down on the edge of the rug at the doorway. She sank onto the couch at an angle from Mamie's chair, then looked up at the hovering Teddi.

"Thank you, Teddi, is it? I think Mamie and I can manage by ourselves now, if you want to run on home."

Teddi sucked in an uncomfortable breath. "I am home. I live here now."

"Oh." Dora was disconcerted. "I'm sorry, I thought you

were a neighbor." She forgot about Teddi, and leaned forward to cover Mamie's hand where it rested on the arm of the rocker. "We'll have to comfort each other," she said. "It's so hard to believe, isn't it? That Ricky's gone. He was so . . . so *vital*. . . ."

She stopped, groped in the pocket of her maternity dress for a handkerchief, and pressed it to her face, overcome with emotion.

"We held a memorial service for him last week. Thursday," Mamie said faintly. "At our church, where he used to go to Sunday school when he was a little boy."

The handkerchief came down and was twisted between Dora's fingers. "It's such a pity his body wasn't recovered. That there can't even be a grave to visit."

"My . . . my husband doesn't have a grave, either," Mamie managed. "He wanted to be cremated and have his ashes scattered up in the mountains, where he loved to hike."

"Does it bother you," Dora asked earnestly, "that he doesn't have a grave?"

"No." Mamie spoke softly. "Now I feel that he's . . . everywhere. Anyplace I go."

Dora nodded. "Yes. I can see that. How sad, to lose first a husband and now a son." She drew in a deep breath, and again patted her belly. "I hope . . . I hope it will be some consolation to you now that you will have a grandchild. It's a boy. We talked about naming him and decided on Daniel Richard Thrane, and I guess that's what I'll go with. Unless you'd particularly like his first name to be the same as his father's? A little Ricky?"

Teddi felt as if she were being pelted with stones, none of them big enough to knock her over, but leaving her bruised. She wanted to take Mamie off in another room, to hug her, to give her time to assimilate this unexpected turn of events.

There was no question but that all the pain had come rushing back, the pain that had begun the moment the call had come from the airline and had lasted right on through the services at the church, where old friends from years back had hugged Mamie and squeezed her hands, and murmured words of condolence. They had brought food to the house, just as other neighbors had done when Teddi's mother had died. And now, when the grief hadn't even really subsided yet, it was being resurrected.

The idea of a grandson was an unexpected one. Teddi felt rocked back on her heels, and she could see that Mamie was considerably more shaken than she was herself.

Dora was waiting for a response, but as yet Mamie was incapable of deciding on a name for a grandchild she'd just learned about. Dora looked up at Teddi.

"I wonder if I might use your bathroom? I'm at a stage where I need to go about every half hour. That's normal during pregnancy."

"Yes, of course," Teddi said, and led the way down the hallway.

She decided she didn't need to wait for Dora to relieve herself. She could easily find her way back to the living room. Teddi returned to Mamie's side and sank onto her knees at Mamie's feet.

Mamie's lips were trembling as she closed a hand around Teddi's when it was offered.

"Ricky's wife," she said. "I never dreamed he had gotten married. I can't imagine why he didn't write and tell me that."

"Ricky never wrote very often," Teddi reminded her. Yet from the look of Dora, she was very close to delivering her baby, which meant that the marriage had probably taken place quite a while ago. And there were telephones. Wouldn't you think Ricky would have been proud enough to have called his mother and told her that she was to become a grandmother?

Down the hallway, the toilet flushed.

Teddi wished desperately that she could think of something helpful to say, but all she could do was cling to Mamie's hand.

Clearly Dora had come to stay. The two suitcases stood as silent testimony to that. And she'd said, "I was hoping to find a family here."

What did that do to Teddi's own prospects for staying here in Mamie's house?

Chapter 2

TEDDI HAD BEEN LIVING with Mamie for only the past four months. Before that, she'd lived next door since she was six years old.

Mamie and Mrs. Stuart, Teddi's mom, hadn't been close friends. They were, after all, a generation apart in age. But they'd been cordial, calling out greetings, accepting package deliveries for one another, sometimes talking about the flowers and vegetables that Mamie raised.

That time seemed far in the distant past. Before her mom got sick, Teddi hadn't found it necessary to seek out another mother figure, but she and Mamie had been friendly enough. Once in a while Mamie had hired her to help pull weeds, which they had done together. After an hour or two in the hot sun, Mamie had invited her inside for a cold drink before she went home.

When Gloria Stuart was diagnosed with cancer and became unable to do all the things she'd done earlier, however, the situation had changed.

Everybody in the neighborhood had rallied around with casseroles and cakes and offers to run errands. Nobody was more attentive than Mamie, though she'd kept it all low-key.

"I had extra asparagus and thought you might like some," she'd say, popping in with a small casserole dish. Or, "I baked bread today and thought you might like a loaf."

Occasionally, when Teddi was coming home from school, Mamie would call out to her from the doorway, "Cookie day, Teddi. Would you like a few?"

At first Teddi had simply eaten the cookies and gone home. Gradually milk was added to the cookies, and during periods when her mother had to be hospitalized, she joined Mamie for simple suppers because her father stayed with his wife.

And gradually, too, they'd talked and begun to share their lives.

Ricky was still living at home until about a year and a half ago. He was a tall, dark, good-looking guy, always joking and teasing when he saw her. He was a lot older than Teddi, so he didn't really pay special attention to her, of course.

She'd had a crush on him since she was about eleven, in that silly hopeless way little girls have. One day he'd given her a ride home when it was raining, and insisted on treating her to a hot chocolate because, he said, *he* wanted one.

He hadn't talked down to her because he was twelve years older. Teddi appreciated that.

Although it didn't happen often, Teddi was pleased when Ricky was home when she went over to see Mamie. Even with the difference in their ages, they discovered they liked a lot of the same books, though Ricky had outgrown some of them. Still, he remembered how he'd cherished the best of them, and he was willing to talk about them while Teddi was discovering them.

Once, she sat behind him at the movies when he was with a pretty girl. She was distracted from the screen by his profile when he turned to the girl, and by his laughter, which was contagious.

And then, during a romantic scene in glowing Technicolor, she had watched as Ricky bent his head and kissed the girl.

Teddi felt her stomach twist with a sensation she'd never experienced before. She envied the girl. Someday, she hoped, a boy would kiss her that way.

It was disappointing when Ricky left home, though of course she'd always known he'd never pay any real attention to her. Mamie told her he'd gotten a job in San Diego.

Teddi remembered how happy Mamie had been to get a letter from him. "He's not much for writing," she confessed. "His dad was like that, too."

Teddi'd sort of hoped that someday he'd come back to Marysville and stay. Maybe, by then, twelve years' difference in age wouldn't matter so much.

Of course he never had, and now he never would. Instead there was Dora.

Dora was a totally unexpected development. She was rather quiet, and after she'd rested a bit there was more color in her cheeks, making her more attractive.

She was commendably solicitous of Mamie. "Would you like to rest a bit? I guess my coming here was really a shock."

Mamie, who never rested in the daytime, agreed. "Maybe I will lie down for half an hour or so."

Dora's smile encouraged her. "I'm tired, too. Being pregnant is exhausting. Would you show me where I'll be sleeping?"

The words jolted Teddi anew. Clearly Dora was taking it for granted that she was staying, moving in with Mamie.

"I had thought maybe . . . Ricky's old room?" Dora suggested.

Teddi felt prickles along her arms, as if a cold wind had blown over her.

"Well, Teddi's in Ricky's old room now," Mamie said uncertainly. Mamie was almost never uncertain about anything.

"Oh." The word was heavy with disappointment. "Well . . ."

Teddi didn't want to say anything, but she didn't want Mamie put on the spot, either. "There's that storage room upstairs," she said. "That could be cleaned out."

Dora proffered a grateful smile. "You wouldn't mind moving up there? Stairs aren't so handy for someone who's pregnant. Especially with my getting up so often during the night."

So it was Teddi who adjusted, of course. What else could she do?

Even before she moved out of Ricky's room—which she had come to think of as *her* room—Dora took a nap on Teddi's bed.

"You don't mind, do you? I'm just awfully tired. A nap before supper would be wonderful."

So Teddi went upstairs and surveyed the room that had never been intended for much more than a storage place.

At one time Ricky and his older brother, Ned, had played up there on rainy days. In Washington State there were a lot of those.

Today was sunny, but the windows hadn't been washed in years, so it was gloomy enough to be a rainy day. Luckily Mamie hadn't stored a whole lot of stuff in the room, or clearing it out would have been a problem.

There were half a dozen cardboard cartons, marked CHRISTMAS DECORATIONS and SUMMER CLOTHES and RICKY'S STUFF. There was an old-fashioned radio in a tall cabinet, a chair with a broken leg, and a bed.

It was Ned's bed, dismantled and moved up after Ned had left for college, so that Ricky would have more room in the quarters they had shared downstairs.

The mattress and springs leaned against the wall, covered with an old sheet to keep them from getting dirty. Nevertheless, when Teddi pulled off the sheet, dust rose in a cloud that made her sneeze.

She needed dust cloths and some soap and water, she supposed, sighing. She wondered if the windows could be opened enough so she could reach outside and clean them.

Amazingly enough, both of them slid free after only a moment of resistance, letting in some welcome fresh air.

Teddi went back downstairs to get rags and a bucket of water and detergent. The house was quiet. Mamie's door was closed, with only silence behind it.

The door to her own room—now *Dora's* room—wasn't quite shut, and through the narrow crack Teddi saw Ricky's wife stretched out on the blue-and-white spread.

Dora looked very young and vulnerable in her sleep. Her hair drifted down over her cheek, and her mouth was slightly open. If it hadn't been for the bulge of her belly, Teddi might have guessed her at about her own age.

How sad it must be, to have lost the husband she loved and to be facing the birth of a baby without him. Without any family at all, apparently, except for a mother-in-law she'd only just met.

Teddi walked quietly, so as not to disturb her, and gathered up her supplies.

There was a package of pork chops defrosting on the drain board when she entered the kitchen. Two chops. Teddi hesitated, then opened the freezer and got out another package. There would be three for supper now.

The upper bedroom wasn't as bad as she'd thought it might be to put in order, though it was awkward reassembling the bed by herself. Under other circumstances she'd have asked Mamie to come up and help haul the springs and mattress onto the frame, but she kept remembering how Mamie had looked when she had gone to her room to rest. Much older than only a few hours earlier, certainly.

Teddi didn't know for sure just how old Mamie was. In her early fifties, probably. The shock of having Dora show up on her doorstep had momentarily aged her beyond that. At least Teddi hoped it would be momentary.

She had to make several trips up and down the stairs. Once for the vacuum cleaner, to get rid of the dust. Then for the mop to wipe off the linoleum that covered the floor. And again for sheets for the bed.

She had brought her own bedding when she'd moved from next door, but it was on the bed downstairs, in the room where Dora was resting. She didn't have another bedspread. Maybe she'd be able to get it later and put Ricky's old spread in its place.

It wasn't very homey in the attic room. There was Sheetrock on the walls, but it had never been papered or painted. She'd have to bring her clothes up, out of the dresser and the closet downstairs, but there wasn't much of any place to hang them or put them away, she thought. She might have to pound some nails into the unfinished walls in lieu of a closet, and maybe the old radio would serve as a place to put stacks of underwear.

The windows were the last thing she cleaned. One of them looked out on the street, the other over the house that for most of her life had been her home.

She stood at that window for a time, remembering.

There had been good times, before her mother got sick.

15

Some people got cancer and died very quickly. It had taken her mom a long time. There hadn't been many good times then. No more games or reading together, or just sharing confidences. The chemo made her mom so sick much of the time that she hadn't been up to doing much of anything. Teddi had prayed and prayed that her mother would get well, but it hadn't happened.

Sometimes, when the pastor or a church member had visited her, Mom had smiled and seemed a little better for a few hours. But the pain always came back; she had grown weaker and weaker, less and less interested in whatever was going on with anything outside her bedroom.

Teddi could see into that room now, because the curtains had been taken down when the room was painted before the house was put on the market. The second floor of that house was on the same level as this attic room at Mamie's. The soft blue carpet was still there. Blue had been Gloria Stuart's favorite color. She had been buried wearing her favorite blue dress. It had been much too big for her, since she had wasted away during the time she was sick, but the funeral director had arranged it so that it didn't seem grotesquely large.

Teddi swallowed the lump in her throat that remembering the funeral always brought, and was turning away from the window when a yellow truck pulled into the driveway next door.

It was one of those trucks that people rent to move their household goods.

As her attention was caught by the new arrival, her recollection of her mother in the flower-shrouded coffin, so pale and unnatural looking, began to fade. She didn't want to remember the funeral. Even after four and a half months, it was still incredibly vivid and painful. She pressed her face against the clean glass to see better.

A man got out of the truck, a rather husky figure in blue jeans and a work shirt. A moment later he was joined by a woman, also in jeans with a flaming orange shirt, and together they went up the steps to the front door. They had a key to open it.

Teddi knew the place had been sold. The realtor had reported that to Mamie. The deal hadn't gone through yet, because the new family needed to get a mortgage, but they also needed to move as soon as possible, so they'd arranged to pay rent for a month or two.

Mamie said that when it sold, Teddi might get a little money out of it. Not much, though, because there were bills to settle first, and the Stuarts hadn't owned the house free and clear. Because of the way her father had died four months ago, only a few weeks after his wife's death, there hadn't been any money from his life insurance, so even a small sum would be welcome. The social services agency paid Mamie to keep Teddi as a foster child, but there were things like shoes and clothes that Teddi needed and didn't think she could ask for. When the house money came, she hoped it would be enough to take care of things like that.

As she watched, a car drove in beside the truck. The driver—who got out, stretched, then opened the back door for a couple of younger children—looked to be in his mid-teens. Sixteen, anyway, because he couldn't have gotten a driver's license before that age.

He was slim hipped, with somewhat bony, wide shoulders under a black T-shirt with some sort of motto on it. From her angle, Teddi couldn't make out what it was.

There was a little girl of about ten, and another of maybe seven. A family. A nice, happy family, Teddi guessed. She wondered if they would be happy in her old home, or if they, too, might face tragedy as the Stuarts had.

At the moment, there was no sadness. The girls were laughing as they walked toward the house. Then the little one ran back to the car and hauled out a small suitcase, bumping it down to the ground.

"Jason! Come help me!" she yelled.

His name was Jason.

"Teddi! Are you up there?"

She heard her own name and turned away from the window. For a moment she felt a touch of warmth, of pleasure in the knowledge that someone who looked pleasant was moving into the house that had stood vacant since the night she had found her father's body.

Probably the realtor hadn't told them about Stan Stuart killing himself in the garage. It wouldn't have been a selling point for the house.

"Teddi?" Mamie called again

"I'm coming," Teddi called back, and started down the stairs. Before she reached the bottom, her fears were once more prickling along her spine.

Chapter 3

"**DID YOU HAVE** a good nap?" Teddi asked as she emerged from the bottom of the stairs.

Mamie stared at her over the basket of lettuce she'd brought in from the garden. "Nap? Oh, dear Lord, I didn't sleep, child! How could I sleep?"

She led the way into the kitchen and started water running into the sink to wash the lettuce. "I made some iced tea; I thought we could have some before we get supper started. Sit down, Teddi, so we can talk."

There were two tall frosty glasses on the table, and a plate of sugar cookies. Another glass, empty, acknowledged the third presence in the house now. When Dora showed up, she would know she'd been expected.

Teddi sank into a chair and took a sip of the tea as Mamie whisked the greens through the water and set them to drain in a colander before she joined Teddi at the table.

"I can hardly form a coherent thought," Mamie said, "before another one pushes it out. I don't know if you can imagine . . ." She pushed back a wisp of hair and sighed. She was obviously very tired, yet there was an undercurrent of excitement, too. "I knew Ned and Leah weren't planning to have a family, even before Ned got hurt in that car wreck. Now with all the reconstructive surgery he's having, the expense will be another reason why they can't afford a family. And they're both too career-oriented, anyway. But I'd hoped Ricky might eventually give me grandchildren. And then, when they called to tell me he'd been on that plane. . . . That was one of the things I thought about, you know. Not only that Ricky was . . . gone, but that there would never be any grandchildren."

She sipped at her tea and reached for a cookie, which she didn't eat but left lying on a napkin, picking at the edges of it so that it crumbled.

If I ever have any kids, Teddi reflected, *they* won't have any *grandparents*. Maybe Mamie would fill in for them.

"And now," Mamie said, "*this*. Dora. It's almost a miracle, isn't it? Not only do I have another daughter-in-law, but she's *pregnant*. I suppose I should tell Ned, but he has so many problems right now, maybe it's better to wait." She sat, clearly pondering an uncertain future.

Teddi cleared her throat. "It seems funny Ricky didn't let you know he'd gotten married and that they were expecting a baby."

"Oh, that's disappointing, yes. But he was never a very

good writer. When he went to camp, when he was nine or ten, the only postcard I got was the one they made him write. And the time he got banged up in that motorcycle accident just after he went to San Diego, when he was hospitalized for five days, he didn't have anyone let me know. And even the good things . . . Ricky didn't always communicate. Did I ever tell you about the trophy he won his last year in high school? For academic excellence! And he never mentioned it! I found it in his room after graduation. Of course, if I hadn't been sick the night of the ceremony, I'd have been there when they presented it to him, I suppose. I felt so bad that I missed his graduation, especially since his father was no longer alive to go. But I was down with the flu."

Mamie laughed a little, fondly, remembering her younger son. "I thought all the possibilities were gone, Teddi, and now I'm going to have a grandson. Isn't it wonderful?"

Dutifully, Teddi nodded, glad that Mamie seemed happy, happier than she had been.

"I wonder if he'll look like Ricky? He was such a pretty baby. Big dark eyes and always plenty of hair, even when he was born."

"Is Dora still sleeping? She must have been very tired."

"She was dead to the world when I peeked in on her a few minutes ago. She's a pretty little thing, isn't she?"

Again Teddi murmured assent. A part of her was alert for any sound from the bedroom that had, until a few hours ago, been hers.

"I'm sorry we had to move you upstairs," Mamie said.

"Was it an awful mess up there?"

"Not too bad. I got the bed up and the dust off things. I don't have anywhere to put my clothes, though, when I move them."

"Why don't you take that clothes rack out of the laundry room? We can get by without it. Maybe we can find a dresser at a garage sale; everybody's having them right now. Keep your eyes open and let me know if you see anything."

That suggested that Dora moving in didn't necessarily mean that Teddi would have to find somewhere else to go. Teddi relaxed, but only fractionally. The situation was still too tense. Who knew what Mamie might think when she'd had time to consider all the possibilities?

Teddi had no family anywhere except three elderly aunts she scarcely knew, living hundreds of miles away in Utah. If she left Mamie's, it meant going to an unknown foster home.

They drank their tea, each of them deep in her own thoughts, and then they worked together to fix supper. Mamie thanked her with a smile for getting out the extra chops. They scrubbed potatoes for baking, made a salad, and Mamie sent Teddi out to pull up a few baby carrots for steaming.

Teddi was setting the table—in the dining room, as for a special occasion—when Dora finally showed up. They heard her go into the bathroom first, and then she came padding out in her stocking feet, red marks of sleep still on one side of her face.

"I hope you had a good nap," Teddi said uncertainly.

"Oh, wonderful. If I hadn't had to go to the bathroom, I probably would still be asleep," Dora confessed. "Now I'm feeling hungry."

"It'll be about twenty minutes, I think. The meat and potatoes are in the oven."

"It sure smells good. Will it be okay if I sit in the living room and watch TV?"

"Sure. Help yourself."

Teddi went back to the kitchen for napkins. "She's up now," she said.

Mamie had her head in the refrigerator. "Good. I hope she's feeling better. Do you think we should have cottage cheese, too? Maybe with pineapple stirred into it?"

They had never, since Teddi had been here, had their cottage cheese jazzed up with pineapple.

They took their places a short time later, with Dora across from Teddi, and Mamie in her customary chair at the end of the table. The aroma drifting up from the chop platter was mouthwatering.

Dora smiled. "Oh, this looks so good!"

Mamie nodded. "Let's bless it, and then we'll dig in."

Obediently, Dora put her hands in her lap and bowed her head. But Teddi had the feeling the girl wasn't used to saying grace.

Mamie didn't settle for the usual brief blessing, either. Instead she added, "And thank you, God, for sending Dora to us, and for the child she will soon have. May she deliver it safely, and have a healthy baby. In Jesus' name, we ask. Amen."

Being pregnant must make an expectant mother extra hungry, Teddy thought as Dora loaded her plate and dug into her food. At one point she asked, "You only have the two bedrooms, then? Aside from the one nobody used, in the attic? Somehow, I pictured you living in a larger house."

"That's right. Rick and Ned always shared the room you're in now, so we never needed a third bedroom."

Teddi felt a twinge of something she couldn't quite identify. Already it was Dora's room, though she herself had not yet moved out of it.

Dora cleaned her plate, then hesitated. "Does anyone want that last chop? I must seem an awful pig, but eating for two seems to do that to me."

"By all means," Mamie told her, handing over the platter, "finish it off."

Teddi hadn't wanted it, but for some reason she felt slightly uncomfortable about Dora finishing off two chops. It wasn't as if two helpings of meat were out of line; in the very old days, when her mom was cooking their meals, her dad often had extra helpings.

In the later stages of Gloria Stuart's illness, many of their meals had consisted of toasted cheese sandwiches and tomato soup, or take-out Chinese or chicken on better days. By that time her mother wasn't interested in either eating or anyone else's nutrition. It had been a joy to eat at Mamie's table, where fruits and vegetables and even the chicken had all been home-cooked.

Dora picked up the chop bone in her fingers to gnaw off the last of the meat, then daintily used her napkin. "That

24

was terrific, Mamie. Ricky always said you were a fabulous cook. He wasn't exaggerating."

Mamie smiled her pleasure. "Why don't you go in the front room and relax now, Dora. Teddi and I will clear away."

As soon as they were finished in the kitchen, Teddi suggested that she use this opportunity to get as much of her stuff out of the downstairs bedroom as she could.

"Good idea," Mamie said, patting her shoulder. "Dora may want to go to bed early."

Teddi was about ready to go to bed, too, by the time she'd run up and down the stairs a dozen times. She lugged the hanging rack up from the laundry room and put her underclothes and T-shirts into paper bags for the time being. Luckily she didn't have all that much to move; she had had new clothes over the past year or so only when she completely outgrew the old ones.

Before what she planned as her final trip for the evening, Teddi went toward the living room to say good night, only to find herself in the middle of a conversation.

"When is the baby due, Dora?" Mamie was asking.

"Within the next week or two, I think. I'd expected to be able to make more preparations for him, but what with losing Ricky . . . well, I didn't get very far."

Teddi, unnoticed in the doorway, thought, *But Ricky only died two weeks ago.* Why had she waited until she was a month from giving birth before she did anything? Didn't people usually start making or buying baby clothes sooner than this?

25

"I don't have anything left from the boys, of course," Mamie said. "I gave everything away years ago. We'll have to start looking. What *do* you have?"

"Nothing, really. Not even diapers. I'd hoped to use disposable ones; they're so much easier, aren't they? And of course I don't have a crib."

"We'll be watching garage sales to find a dresser for Teddi," Mamie told her. "Maybe we can find a used crib, too."

"We were going to buy everything new, seeing that Danny would be our first." Dora sounded wistful.

Mamie laughed. "I don't think we had a thing new when Ned and Ricky were born. Except for handmade gifts the church ladies brought us. The lucky thing about babies is that they don't know the difference between new and used."

"I guess that's true, isn't it? Well, in the long run, I suppose it's a good thing I didn't have much bought for the baby. I couldn't possibly have carried it here with me on the bus, could I?"

"Where did you come from, dear?" Mamie asked, and Teddi hovered, waiting for the answer.

"Where did you last hear from Ricky?" Dora asked.

"Oh, the letter was mailed in San Diego, I think. Is that where you were?"

"Yes. We had an apartment there. I wouldn't have come to you so quickly except that the rent was up on the first of the month, and I didn't really feel I could afford to pay it for another month. We didn't have much of anything in the bank, so I didn't want to waste any of it. I can see now that I've been a shock to you. I should have written, but I couldn't find your address in any of Ricky's things. I just knew the town. I looked you up in the phone book when I got off the bus and I started to call, but then I thought it would be better just to come, as long as I was nearly here. I'm sorry if that turned out to be poor judgment."

"Well, it's turned out all right. Ricky was working, wasn't he?" There was a note of concern in Mamie's voice. "He wrote to me quite a while ago that he'd gotten a job with a computer firm."

"Yes, he did, but they laid him off. He got another job, but not until he'd been out of work for about two months, so we got behind. It's hard to save when the work isn't steady, and you're newly married and need to furnish a whole apartment."

"How well I remember, even though it was almost thirty years ago! Even the price of a set of salt-and-pepper shakers was more than we could manage the first few weeks. If it hadn't been for garage sales and thrift shops, I don't know how we'd have managed." Mamie didn't make it sound as if it had been a hardship, though. She and her husband had been very happy in spite of being poor in their early years; she had told Teddi many stories about it.

If it had been me seeking refuge with a mother-in-law I didn't know, who didn't realize I even existed, I certainly would have contacted her before I came here, to be sure I was welcome.

Teddi bit her lip. Was she being petty simply because her own security was threatened? Mamie didn't really owe *her* anything, the way she did Dora.

27

Dora's words cut through her musings. "If Ricky had worked another month, we'd have had insurance to pay for this baby. I did go to the doctor in San Diego. As it is, I'll probably have to have it at home to be able to afford it."

That made Teddi straighten her spine. Have the baby here, in *her* room?

"Oh, my. Well, that is a complication," Mamie admitted. "It would probably be a good idea to apply for DSHS for the both of you, while there's still time to get the paperwork done."

Dora's words were soft, so that Teddi could barely hear them. "Ricky never wanted us to take charity. He couldn't bear the idea of being on welfare, not just because he was proud, but because of how difficult all that paperwork is. And you have to keep verifying everything, proving you're eligible and all that."

"But you could easily do that," Mamie protested. "After all, your husband just died and you're all alone. Surely they'd help you."

"It's hard to ask strangers for help," Dora murmured.

But she didn't hesitate to come here, to Mamie, and Mamie is a stranger.

But legally Dora's mother-in-law, Teddi amended, trying to be fair.

Mamie spoke with unaccustomed firmness. "It would be foolish not to get proper medical care because of squeamishness over accepting charity. You can prove you were married to my son, can't you?"

Dora moistened her lips. "Oh, yes. I have our marriage certificate. I'll get it and show it to you."

She brushed past Teddi in the doorway to get her purse and handed a folded paper to Mamie. Teddi caught only a glimpse of the document as Mamie looked at it, then handed it back. "Fine," Mamie said. "We'll take this and any other papers you have when we go to the social services office. I don't know if there's ordinarily a waiting period to get help when coming from another state, but surely the fact that you're my daughter-in-law will make a difference when you had nowhere else to go."

Dora put the certificate away, looking dubious. "My husband said . . . I'm not sure he'd want me to go on welfare."

"Let's talk to someone who knows more about such things than we do," Mamie told her. She glanced at Teddi. "Was there something special you wanted, dear?"

"I'll take one more load up with me," Teddi said, "and then I think I'll go to bed."

"Good idea. I guess we're all tired," Mamie said. "It's been an emotional day, and that can wear anyone out."

"It's certainly worn me out," Dora affirmed. "I think I'll wait until tomorrow to unpack my things."

Teddi followed Dora into the downstairs bedroom, feeling very awkward. It was as if she were already intruding on the other girl's territory.

She scooped a book off the night table and some odds and ends off the top of the dresser. Then she reached up to take down the small picture of a woodsy scene, one that her mother had painted many years earlier, before Teddi was born. It was the only picture she had taken with her from the house when she left it.

"Oh," Dora said disappointedly, "are you going to take that? I really like it, and it'll leave a mark if you take it down."

"No, it won't," Teddi said. "It hasn't been up there long enough to have left a spot on the wallpaper."

"But it's so uplifting, don't you think, to be able to see it from the bed that way? I enjoyed it before I fell asleep."

Teddi hesitated, then drew back her hand. Under the circumstances, how could she begrudge the girl such a small thing?

She gathered up a few more articles and, without a further word, left the room. She didn't trust herself to say so much as "good night."

Mamie, who was in the hallway when she came out, ruffled her hair in a tender gesture. "Sleep well, Teddi. We'll have lots to do tomorrow, hitting those garage sales. Good night, Dora."

In the attic bedroom, so alien, so barren, Teddi dumped everything on the floor for lack of a better place, and turned to open a window. In spite of her scrubbing efforts, the place retained a slightly musty smell.

There was a light in the room directly opposite hers, in the old house. The blue carpeting gave it a luxurious air. Teddi wondered which members of the family were going to sleep there.

And then she saw him, the boy, Jason. He was hauling

bedding past the window, until he suddenly noticed her.

He stopped. Teddi was self-conscious, as if she'd been deliberately caught peeking, her hands still on the raised frame of the window.

Jason tossed his bedding off to the side and threw open his own window.

"Hi," he called.

"Hi," Teddi responded.

"Are you the girl who used to live here?"

"Yes."

"The real estate lady told us you'd moved next door. I'm Jason Temple."

"Teddi Stuart."

"Glad to meet you. Maybe you can give us some basic information in the next few days. Like, where's the library?"

Teddi felt some of the tension go out of her as she laughed. "The library *is* pretty basic. It's two blocks down that way, then turn right for—"

"Why don't you show me?" Jason suggested. "Maybe tomorrow afternoon?"

"If I'm not busy with Mamie going to garage sales," Teddi accepted, with a slight fluttering of her pulse. "We have to look for some things tomorrow."

"Any chance you'd like company?" Jason asked. "We have to look for a few things, too. Like some lamps. We had mostly overhead fixtures in the old place, and we need lamps."

"Sure. I'll ask Mamie and let you know."

"Great. See you tomorrow, then."

"Right." There were no shades up here, so Teddi turned off her own light before she got undressed. There was plenty of illumination from the streetlight out front.

For a few moments she had forgotten what Dora's sudden appearance might mean to her own future. For a few moments she'd had something to look forward to, showing a new guy in town where the library was and searching out the garage and yard sales.

It was only when she slid into the unfamiliar bed that she recalled how her life had changed yet again. She wasn't sure the change was going to be for the better.

Chapter 4

TEDDI WOKE FEELING disoriented. For a few seconds she stared at the unfamiliar ceiling, fighting panic, and then she remembered.

Dora had come, and Teddi had been banished to the attic.

She knew what Mamie would say if she were to voice that idea. "Oh, Teddi, don't be silly! You haven't been banished at all! It's just that Dora's pregnant and needs to be near the bathroom. You hardly ever get up at night."

Teddi lay there, reluctant to move. Then she heard shouted voices from next door. "Jason, hurry up!" A male voice responded, and car doors slammed.

There were neighbors in the house that had once been

her home. The Temples. And Jason Temple had asked if he could go with her to the yard sales.

That brought her out of bed, and she quickly dressed in jeans and her best-looking T-shirt, a pale green one with a flower garden motif. She'd have liked one with a funny saying on it, but she didn't have one.

Mamie was in the kitchen, making waffles. Waffles were usually reserved for leisurely Saturday mornings. Of course today they were in honor of Dora.

"Morning, Teddi! Should we have strawberry jam as well as syrup?"

"Why not?" Teddi agreed, and went to get it.

"I see a new family is moving in next door," Mamie told her, pouring more batter into the waffle maker. "They have children."

"Yes. I met the son last night, talked to him when we both opened our windows. His name's Jason Temple. He asked if we'd take him around to the yard sales to see if he could find some lamps."

Mamie grinned at her. "Attractive, is he?"

"I guess so," Teddi said, feeling self-conscious. "Are we all going, you and Dora and me?"

"That might be the best way," Mamie said.

But when she and Teddi had eaten, and there was no sound from Dora's bedroom, Mamie changed her mind. "Here," she said, handing some bills to Teddi, "you and Jason go. See if you can find a baby crib and a dresser. Pay for them, and I'll go back later with the car to pick them up. Dora's still asleep, and I don't feel I can leave her here with

34

no one in the house. If you see any baby clothes, blankets, that kind of thing, get those, too, if they're in good condition. I'll get some new things next time I get to town."

It felt strange to be walking up to ring the bell at the house where she'd lived for so long, but she didn't have to. Jason came out before she got there.

"Dad says I can take the car, so we don't have to try to carry stuff home. What do we do, just drive around looking for SALE signs?"

"No, I've got a list of places from the paper," Teddi said. "There'll probably be other ones, too, so we'll watch for them. I thought we'd start with this one; it's only two blocks away."

It turned out to be a fun morning. Jason was good company, and he made her laugh when he held up one of the ugliest lamps she'd ever seen, asking her opinion, and when he talked about his family.

She would like the Temples, Teddi thought. The little sisters were Annie, who was ten, and Heidi, who was seven. Annie was the quiet, serious one, and Heidi never stopped talking.

"Never," Jason said solemnly. "Even in her sleep. When I want to read, I have to hide in my room to get away from her."

"I always wanted a sister," Teddi told him, scanning tables of odds and ends.

"I'll give you one of mine. Especially if you take Heidi. Oh, hey, look at this! I'll bet Annie would love it." He held up a small straw hat decorated with bobbing cherries. He read the price tag. "Fifty cents." The lady on the other side of the table was watching him, and he grinned at her. "Make it a quarter and I'll take it."

"Sold," the lady said, and he perched it on his head so that he still had his hands free.

"Very becoming," Teddi told him, laughing again. "That was a bargain."

"Half the fun of these things is that almost everybody is willing to negotiate. I don't see any decent lamps, but there's a dresser. You want to look at it?"

On close inspection, the dresser was in bad shape. But as they made their way around to the sales listed in the paper, they saw a number of others. Teddi settled for the cheapest one that looked okay, and Jason wrestled it into the car.

Nearly every sale had baby clothes, but most of them had stains or were worn out. There were no cribs, though they did find a bassinet that was in pretty good condition.

"Five dollars," Teddi mused. "If I buy it, will I have enough left when I come to a good crib?"

"Offer her two," Jason advised, and to Teddi's delight, the lady took the money. The bassinet, too, went into the car.

It was late morning when they came across a pair of tall, elegant table lamps. The sticker said, PAIR $15. Jason got them for ten. "Now all we need is a baby crib, right?"

"Right. But the bassinet may work for a little while, if we can't find the bed."

"This is for a little tiny baby, right?" Jason asked, stowing the lamps without their shades in the backseat.

"He isn't even born yet. But I guess he's due soon."

"Whose baby is it?"

Jason paused to open the door for her, then went around the car to his own side.

"Dora's. She was Ricky's wife, Mamie's younger son. He was killed in an airplane crash two weeks ago."

Jason sobered. "Wow. That's a bummer. She going to live with you?"

"She showed up yesterday, so it looks like it. Mamie didn't even know Ricky had gotten married."

"He never even told her he got married? Boy, my mom would kill me if I did anything like that." Then he flushed. "Sorry, that was a stupid remark, wasn't it? Where do we go next?"

At the last planned stop before they went home for lunch, they finally located a crib.

Teddi stared at it in disappointment. "It's pretty ugly, isn't it? Dora was hoping to have a new one, but she can't afford it right now."

Jason shook the small bed. "It's sturdy, though. A kid could jump up and down in it and it wouldn't fall apart. You know, a coat of paint would probably make it look fine."

"You think so?" A smiling lady in a pink smock approached them. "You want the crib? It's a steal at that price. New ones cost three times that much."

"Yeah," Jason conceded, "but they don't look like they've been beaten to death."

The lady's smile wavered. "Three of my kids have used

37

it," she admitted, "but it's still useful. Is it for yourselves?"

Teddi's face flamed, but she couldn't think of anything to say except, "No."

Jason, however, was not stumped. "With a coat of paint it might not be bad. Tell you what, you knock twenty-five dollars off that price, and we'll take it and paint it, okay?"

To Teddi's surprise—and relief—they made the deal. The crib had to be dismantled to get it into the car, where it filled up all the space there was left.

"You're amazing," Teddi admitted, sliding into the passenger seat. "I'd never have had the nerve to talk everybody down on the prices like that. You saved me quite a bit."

"They expect you to haggle. They set their prices in the first place to allow for it. You know, this was fun," Jason said as they headed for home. "Would you have time this afternoon to show me where the library is?"

"Sure, if Mamie doesn't have something else planned for me to do," Teddi said, and hoped Mamie wouldn't.

Jason brought in the dresser, then carried in the crib parts while Teddi managed the bassinet, setting them on Mamie's back porch. Mamie came out to inspect them and was introduced to Jason.

"I'll set it up again, and then we can paint it," he explained. "We could probably paint that basket thing, too. It'll look fine when that's done."

Dora, however, who obviously had not been up very long, stared dubiously at their purchases. "That crib's pretty old," she commented.

"Old, but sturdy," Jason asserted. "On the way back

from the library we'll stop and get some paint, okay? Now I have to show Mom her new lamps. And give Annie her hat."

Teddi had a sudden thought. "You bought something for Annie, but not for Heidi. Won't she feel slighted?"

Jason stopped on the bottom step. "You're right. She probably will. Hmmm."

"Heidi's the little one?" Mamie asked. "Wait a minute, maybe I've got something."

She vanished inside and came back a few minutes later holding a ceramic cow. "My friends know I collect cows and things with cow motifs. They bring me new ones when they go on vacations. I have two just alike of these. Would she appreciate a cow bank?"

Hopeful, Jason took the cow and headed for home across the backyard. The others went inside for lunch. Mamie smiled brightly at the two girls. "I hope tuna fish sandwiches are okay for this afternoon?"

"Sure," Teddi said, but Dora smiled apologetically. "I'm afraid not any kind of fish agrees with me right now."

"Oh. Well, we'll find something else," Mamie said immediately. "I remember being sensitive to various things when I was pregnant, too. Especially bacon; couldn't stand the smell of it. I was lucky; all sensitivities were gone after the first few months."

They settled on chicken noodle soup, eaten mostly in silence. Mamie tried to keep conversation going by asking questions, most of which Dora answered in monosyllables.

At the end of the meal, Dora pushed back her chair

awkwardly and stood up. "I don't suppose you have a heating pad or a hot water bottle, do you? I woke up with a backache, and it just won't go away."

"I'll get my heating pad," Mamie offered at once.

Teddi had arranged to meet Jason in an hour for their excursion to the library. She thought she had time to read the rest of her borrowed book before then, so she went to get it.

She'd left it on the coffee table in the living room, but it wasn't there.

"What are you looking for, dear?" Mamie asked as she handed over the heating pad to Dora, who was stretched out on the couch.

"My book. The one with the picture of a blond girl on the cover, with a dog."

"Oh, is this it?" Dora asked, and there the book was, in her hands. "I picked it up just before lunch and started reading it. It's quite good. You don't mind if I finish it before you take it back, do you? I won't take very long. I'm a fast reader."

Nonplussed, Teddi swallowed and stared at her. She saw that Mamie was somewhat startled, too, but she left the decision up to Teddi.

Would she seem a total creep if she insisted on having the book back?

Teddi wanted to say that she had to return it to the library day after tomorrow, and she'd really like to finish it today, but somehow her tongue refused to form the words.

In fact, she couldn't say *any* words. She murmured

something unintelligible and turned away, leaving the room.

She told Jason about it as they left a short time later. He regarded her with level dark eyes.

"Do I get the feeling you don't like this Dora very much?" he asked bluntly.

Teddi felt the heat in her face. "That makes me sound pretty . . . petty, doesn't it?"

"I don't know. Maybe not. We have a rule in our house: Nobody can pick up a book someone else is reading until the first person is finished with it. Mom says they almost came to blows about that when they were first married, because Dad would pick up anything lying around wherever she had left it open and start reading it. Then she'd either have to wait until he was through with it or feel guilty for demanding it back. Either way, she said it made her angry. Now she's got a red leather bookmark, and if it's in any book, the rest of us leave it alone."

"Sounds like a good system. I wish I'd thought of it and explained it to Dora yesterday," Teddi said, feeling guilty.

Three days later, she was still feeling guilty about one thing after another.

She'd felt violated when she'd entered the bathroom— after waiting over half an hour while Dora took a long soak (were you supposed to do that when you were expecting a baby practically any minute?)—and then found the container empty when she went to pour out some of her favorite bubble bath.

It was a bottle that had been her mother's, one she'd

41

always associated with the fragrance of her mom. She'd hoarded it, using it sparingly, because she didn't have the money to buy any more. Teddi swallowed her disappointment and took a bath with plain old soap.

Because she knew Mamie didn't care for dirty dishes sitting around, she picked up the odd coffee cups and sandwich plates Dora left in the living room and disposed of her apple cores, including one that had stood overnight and was covered with ants when Teddi discovered it. There was a trail of them straight through from the kitchen that required getting out a can of insect spray.

At least that time Mamie advised Dora it wasn't safe to leave anything around that could draw ants, and Dora promised to be more careful.

Teddi was cleaning up the kitchen after supper that evening when Dora came out for a drink of water, then stood watching as the younger girl wiped off counters and the stove.

"How long have you lived with Mamie?" she asked.

"About four months." Teddi swallowed. "My mother died first, and then my dad. We lived next door, and I'd known Mamie for a long time."

"Did you know Ricky, too?"

"Yes. He was a lot older than I was."

"And you were alone when your dad died? You don't have any other family?"

"No," Teddi said around the lump in her throat. The old aunts didn't count; she'd only met them a couple of times, and they'd never shown any interest in her.

"I don't have any family, either. My dad deserted us when I was a little girl, and then my mom was killed in a street accident. Run down when she was walking home from work."

Dora was making an effort to be friendly. It seemed only reasonable to be responsive.

Teddi made herself think quickly, to sound friendly. "Do you have any brothers or sisters?"

"No. I don't have a soul except for Danny." She rested a hand on her protruding belly. "And now Mamie. Thank God for Mamie. She's a dear, generous person, isn't she?"

"Yes, she is."

"I wish Ricky had told her about me. About us."

"It's funny he didn't," Teddi said, then wondered if that was less than tactful.

"He didn't like writing letters," Dora said, sighing. "How lucky for you, too, that Mamie took you in. So you intend to stay here? You won't be moving on?"

"I have nowhere else to go," Teddi said, still fighting the lump.

"We have something in common, then, don't we?" Dora gave her a small smile. "We're both alone. It's a scary thing, to be alone, especially with a baby coming."

Once the kitchen was in order, they joined Mamie in the living room, where she was reading the paper. She put it down and smiled up at them.

"It's time we had a talk, don't you think? I need to know details . . . how you and Ricky met, what your lives have been like. What he did during the past year or so, when I didn't hear much from him."

"I'm sorry about that. I guess I should have tried to get him to write to you more, but I don't have anyone to write letters to, and I just didn't think about it." Dora sank onto the couch. "You know what I'd really enjoy? Having you tell me all about Ricky as a little boy, as a young man. He never talked much about himself, and there are so many things I don't know about. Do you have pictures of him when he was little? I never saw any pictures of how he looked before I met him."

"Actually, there are snapshots in that big album right over there," Mamie said. "See, the dark red one. Why don't I get it down, and we'll sit on the couch, all three of us, and I'll tell you about the pictures."

So they did. Mamie sat in the middle, turning the pages, pointing out her husband, Greg, then Ned as a baby, and then Ricky.

Dora studied the studio portrait of Ricky when he was a year old. "I hope Danny looks like him," she said softly. "He was so cute."

It seemed very strange to Teddi to sit looking at photographs of a child, and then a young man, who was no longer living. She wondered how Mamie could bear to do it, and then realized that there were tears running down Mamie's cheeks, though her voice was steady. Her own eyes were blurry, too.

Dora ran her fingers over Ricky's first-grade school picture. "Thank you for taking us in, Mamie. I would be so frightened if I were alone, with the baby coming."

For long seconds Mamie hesitated, as if she, too, like

Teddi, had uncertainties. Then she said slowly, "There's nothing to be afraid of, Dora. "We'll take good care of you, won't we, Teddi?"

They spent more than an hour poring over the photo album, and Mamie told stories about her boys as youngsters, some of them very funny. Dora laughed sometimes, and so did Mamie, but Teddi found laughing a hard thing to do when her eyes were so full of tears. And as Mamie was putting the album away, Teddi watched her, and thought that Mamie looked lost and torn about these recent events. As if she, also, struggled with doubts.

But Mamie voiced none of the misgivings Teddi was feeling. If she did, indeed, have them, perhaps it was too much to expect that she would share them with a fourteen-year-old girl who was, after all, only a foster child. Mamie had adult friends to talk to if she needed counsel, if she had questions about Dora that were unanswered except by that totally unexpected marriage certificate.

As she climbed the stairs, Teddi thought that if she were in Mamie's position, she might investigate Dora more thoroughly before offering her unqualified acceptance. But she could not bring herself to say so. Mamie was the adult; she was far more competent than Teddi to determine the truth of matters, and it was her own business if she chose not to discuss any of it with a kid who wasn't even related to her.

She continued to feel the sting of tears as she undressed and got into bed, feeling confused and uncertain and afraid of what the future would hold.

Chapter 5

THE CRIB AND BASSINET turned out very well. Dora inspected them while Teddi held her breath, then smiled. "They look almost new!" she approved. Dora followed Jason as he wheeled the crib into her room.

Mamie cast a look at Teddi as they joined them. "She's so brave, isn't she? Not a tear out of her, with all she's been through."

I'd be crying buckets if my husband had just died, Teddi thought. She didn't say it, though. Mamie was looking happy for the first time since Ricky's plane had crashed into the Pacific. If Dora and a soon-to-be grandson could make her happy, all the better.

It helped some that Jason had moved in next door. Neither of them had shades on their bedroom windows, so if they retired at anywhere near the same time of evening—and Teddi quickly learned that to be around ten P.M.—they talked between their houses.

"I guess I'll have to find something for a shade," Teddi said ruefully. "It doesn't seem quite decent to look into a guy's bedroom, or to have him look into mine."

"I noticed some shades at one of those yard sales. Want to check it out?"

"Sure," Teddi agreed readily.

They found shades to fit their windows at their first stop, and Teddi found a chair, and they looked at all kinds of furniture and junk. Once, she paused before a jewelry display with old-fashioned brooches and necklaces and rings.

One of the latter was obviously a wedding ring, a plain gold band like the one Dora wore.

"I wonder why they're selling it," Teddi mused, picking it up to look at it. "Inside it says G.H. TO V.S. What do you suppose happened to V.S.?"

Jason was more interested in a gigantic squirt gun, which he thought might interest Heidi. But he was polite enough to respond to her casual comment. "If she died, they'd probably have left the ring on her finger, if she didn't have a relative who wanted it. So maybe they were divorced, and the ring didn't have any sentimental value."

"I have my mom's ring. They said it was senseless to throw it away. Sad things happen a lot, don't they?"

"Yeah. Listen, you going to take that chair? I can probably carry it home."

"Okay. I think I can afford it if they'll shave a little off the sticker price."

Jason laughed. "You're getting the idea! Make them an offer. If they won't accept it, then pay the full price, but not before you've tried for a better one."

The sticker on the ring said $2.00. She had had no idea how cheaply some things could be obtained.

Of course, unless a thing was cheap, there was no way Teddi would ever buy it. "One good thing about Dora coming," she observed, "is that it made Mamie think about giving me an allowance. She realized Dora needs money for personal items and has no income, so she's going to pay her a little bit every week. She apologized because she hadn't thought of doing the same for me, so now I have an allowance, too. When the money comes in on the house, maybe I'll have a little of my own."

They carried home their latest purchases, stopping to rest a couple of times because the chair was heavier than they'd thought. Teddi didn't care. It made it take longer, and they laughed a lot.

Later that day, when she was dusting off the big photo album, something occurred to her. Dora was listlessly paging through a magazine, but lifted her head when Teddi spoke.

"You know, I think Mamie would like to have a copy of any picture you have of Ricky. It would have to be newer than any of the ones *she* has."

"Oh. Well, actually, I don't have any pictures of him," Dora confessed. "We never got around to taking any."

"You have none at all? So the baby will never know what his daddy looked like?"

"Maybe Mamie will give me an extra of one of hers," Dora said.

But Dora had not asked for one when they came across duplicates in the loose snapshots, or when they looked at Ricky's graduation picture. Teddi knew there were several of those.

I'd have asked for a graduation picture, Teddi thought.

"She probably will," Teddi said. "It's too bad you didn't have a newer one."

"Yes. You never expect anything bad to happen to a young, healthy man. So you don't do things like take pictures," Dora said sadly.

Gradually they were getting used to each other. Dora never offered to help with any of the household chores, but considering how pregnant she was, that was probably natural. She couldn't bend over to tie shoes, so she wore slip-ons all the time, and if she dropped anything, she just about had to wait for someone else to pick it up.

Dora had bought some delightful-smelling bath oil. Teddi looked at the pink bottle with the gold lettering, tempted to try some of it, but she didn't. She felt guilty even thinking about it, in spite of the fact that Dora had used the last of her own.

Mamie went to town and returned with packages of diapers, baby shirts and gowns, bibs, and three cute little outfits of knitted shirts and pants. One of them had a baseball cap to go with a uniform. "I hit a sale!" she said cheerfully.

Mamie watched Dora open everything and laughed. "This was far more fun than shopping for my own boys. They didn't have all this cute stuff then."

"They're beautiful," Dora said, smoothing out a bib made like the front of a tuxedo, complete with a black bow tie. "Thank you, Mamie."

Teddi stared down at them. "They're so tiny. It doesn't seem as if anyone could ever be small enough to fit into them."

"He probably won't fit into them for long," Mamie predicted. "Babies grow so fast. I bought six months' size, so they'll probably only fit him for a little while. They may be too big to start with, though."

Teddi and Mamie always went to church, but Dora declined to go with them.

"I'm so awkward and uncomfortable," she protested. "I'll just stay home and get a little extra rest, if that's all right."

Mamie, smiling, rested a palm on Dora's belly. "Fine. You just take extra good care of my grandson."

One evening ten days after Dora came, Mamie went out to a church meeting. "We're making a quilt to be auctioned off to raise funds for our missionaries. We're trying to finish it, so I may be late getting back. Just lock up when you go to bed, girls, and I'll use my key."

Right after she left, Dora turned on the TV and watched a game show. People on the screen were jumping up and down and hugging each other as they won cash prizes. Teddi decided she'd rather read, which she could do better upstairs. She made a sandwich to take with her.

Just as she passed the telephone on the hall table, though, it rang.

"Hello?"

"Teddi? I'm going to be delayed even later than I thought," Mamie said. "I'm going over to help Myra Jenkins hang some new curtains and visit with her for a while. She's depressed because of her husband's illness and wants to talk to someone. Don't wait up for me."

Teddi had no sooner hung up than the phone rang again and a different voice responded to her own.

"Hi. I've got to pick up a prescription from the drugstore. Would you like to walk over there with me?" Jason asked. "I understand they sell good ice-cream cones."

"I'd love to," Teddi said, and then blushed. Did she sound too eager? She'd never been on a date. Of course this wasn't a *date,* exactly, just a walk to the drugstore.

She stuck her head around the corner, looking in on Dora. "I'm going out for a little while. Walking over to the mini-mall. Will you be okay by yourself?"

"Of course," Dora said, not taking her eyes off the screen. "Have fun."

Teddi *did* have fun. She pointed out directions to places like the high school, where she and Jason would both be going in September, and the park, where they sat in swings to eat their triple-dip butter pecan cones.

"They have public tennis courts," Jason observed, curling his tongue around a trickle of ice cream down the side of his cone. "You play?"

She shook her head. "No. I never learned how."

"You want to? I could teach you. I've been looking around for a part-time summer job, but I haven't found anything. And Dad wants me to do some things around the new house, anyway, but it won't take me all day, every day. How about it?"

"I'm not very athletic," Teddi said uncertainly. She couldn't believe this very attractive boy was actually issuing such an invitation.

"You'll never get any more so until you try. How about tomorrow morning? Ten o'clock, before it gets too hot."

"Okay," she decided. "If it's okay with Mamie."

They finished their cones, washed off their sticky hands in the fountain in the middle of the park, and headed for home, both content to walk slowly.

As they neared a service station two blocks from home, Jason said suddenly, "Isn't that your Dora?"

"She's not *my* Dora, she's Mamie's," Teddi said automatically, but came to a standstill. "What's she doing making a phone call from there instead of using the phone at home?"

"Probably just wanted to get a breath of fresh air, maybe a little exercise," Jason said. "Hey, what do you say we drop off this prescription at home for Mom and then go back to the high school? We can walk around it, check it out. You can explain where everything is."

"This will be my first term there, too," Teddi admitted. "I'm only a freshman."

"Okay. So we'll explore together. All right?"

So that's what they did. Not that they were able to determine much except where the gym was, and the library building. It didn't matter. It was a pleasure to spend time with someone young, someone who had the power to make her laugh. She hadn't laughed much for quite a long while.

They finally walked home again in the dusk, once more passing the service station. There was the phone booth, and seeing it brought a sudden question to Teddi's mind.

"I wonder who Dora was calling? I mean, she said she didn't have any family, and she hasn't met anyone in town since she got here."

It was a puzzle neither of them could figure out. And when Teddi entered the house a short time later, the TV was off, and there were no lights on anywhere except in the bathroom.

"Dora?" she called out, resolving to ask about the phone call. After all, Dora lived here now; Mamie wouldn't object to her using the phone.

Only the question never got asked.

Dora opened the bathroom door and panted rather than said, "Oh, Teddi, thank goodness you're back!"

Her face was sweating, and her hair stuck to her head. "Help me, Teddi, I'm having the baby."

Chapter 6

DORA'S THIN FINGERS, surprisingly strong, curled around her wrists, drawing her into the lighted bathroom against her will.

Teddi resisted, but Dora was stronger than she was.

"You'll have to help me," Dora panted. "Mostly I should be able to do it myself, but I need you to help. I found sheets and scissors and a blanket to wrap the baby in, but . . ."

She paused, gasping for breath, digging her grip into Teddi's flesh. "Oh, it's happening faster than I expected, oh, oh!"

Teddi struggled to free herself. "I'll call 911 and get an aid car right away to take you to the hospital. . . ."

"No! No, haven't you been listening to what I've been

saying? No hospital! I don't have any insurance, or any money, either! I'll have the baby right here at home; thousands of women have delivered at home, or even out in the fields—oh, oh!"

Panic swept over Teddi as she kept on trying to pull free. She never would have dreamed that Dora had so much strength. What would Mamie do if she were here? Wouldn't she insist on an ambulance, or at least paramedics with an aid car? Where was Mamie? Surely she'd be home soon!

Dora's face, up close this way, had a greasy sheen, but she seemed more excited than frightened.

"I read all about it. I can do it. Spread out the sheets on the bed, folded up so they'll be thick under my hips ... oh! OH!"

Teddi managed to get one hand free and scrabbled for the telephone on the table just outside the bathroom door. She had punched in the nine when Dora struck her wrist a stunning blow, knocking the receiver out of her hand. It slammed against the wall, then swung free.

Babies didn't come within minutes, did they? Teddi looked desperately toward the front door, seeking Mamie. Mamie would know what to do, which was more than Teddi did.

"Hadn't you better lie down?" she asked anxiously.

"No, no, not yet! My water broke, but I don't need to push yet. It'll go faster if I can walk around first. Walk with me, Teddi!"

"I can't prepare the bed if you're hanging on to me," Teddi said. "Look, Dora, I don't know anything about delivering a baby—"

"You don't have to." Dora was between contractions now, though still breathing heavily. "Having a baby is perfectly natural. Nature takes care of the whole thing."

To Teddi's astonishment, the other girl reached out and pulled the phone cord out of the wall. "Now, forget about calling anybody, and just do what I say."

Did she have any choice? She could plug the phone back in, if Dora didn't keep her from doing it, but Dora was determined. Teddi allowed herself to be maneuvered toward Dora's bedroom door, muttering a prayer under her breath as she flicked on the light.

Please, please, let Mamie come home quickly! Dear God, I don't want to do this! I think Dora's crazy!

Crazy or not, Dora forced her inexorably toward the bed. Hands shaking, Teddi unfolded the sheets enough to spread them over the middle of the bed.

What else were you supposed to do to get ready to deliver a baby? "Hot water, aren't you supposed to heat water?" Teddi asked, perturbed beyond being able to figure out what it was for.

"We don't have to heat water these days," Dora told her. "It comes out of the faucet as hot as you can put your hands in. Here, I found a bottle of alcohol. Hold out your hands and I'll pour it over them, so they'll be sterilized. Over the towel, like this."

Teddi felt as if she'd fallen asleep with her eyes open and was now caught in a whirlwind of nightmare. This couldn't be happening.

Yet she felt the cool wetness of the alcohol and the

roughness of the towel, and again she tried to pull free.

"I can't do this, Dora, I don't know how!"

Dora doubled over with another contraction, gripping Teddi's arm painfully, then gasping with relief when the pain had subsided.

"I'll do it. All you have to do is be here and catch the baby when he comes out, and make sure he starts breathing. You know how to do that, don't you? Hold him up by his ankles and swat him on the bottom so he cries. You must have seen it in the movies dozens of times."

She had, but she didn't want to do it. Only there was no opportunity to escape. The baby was coming, and there was only Teddi to do something about it, unless . . . "I could run next door and get Jason's mother," she suggested eagerly.

"No. She'd only call for an ambulance, and it's already too late for that even if I wanted one . . . oh, help me up on the bed!"

Teddi went into a sort of trance from that point on. It was obvious that Dora was in pain during the contractions, especially when she began to push, but she stayed in control. And while in a way Teddi thought the whole procedure would never end, she found no way to free herself to go for help.

By this time Mamie must have helped hang her friend's curtains, and they'd had time for a cup of tea and some talk. Surely she would walk in any minute and take charge.

But Mamie didn't come.

The baby didn't come right away, either, though Dora seemed to be working hard. During the contractions she gripped Teddi's hands painfully, and between them she continued to cling too tightly to allow for escape.

"Please," Teddi begged. "Let me call for help!"

Dora, gritting her teeth and squeezing so hard Teddi thought her bones must be cracking, refused to consider it. "I can't go to the hospital," she gasped.

"That's crazy," Teddi argued. "Mamie said they'd take care of you there. You can prove who you are, and even if social services hasn't done any paperwork on you, they can see you're having a baby! They'll help you, Dora!"

How long it went on, Teddi couldn't be sure. Like Dora, she was sweating and breathing heavily, and she knew her hands and arms were going to be sore where Dora's fingers had dug into them. Once when Dora's grip relaxed momentarily, Teddi made it to the doorway. She grabbed for the disconnected phone, but she had no chance to plug it in.

With a growl like an animal, Dora came off the bed and pursued her, slamming her against the wall as she snatched the phone out of Teddi's grasp.

She doubled over almost immediately, going to her knees with the telephone wrapped by her curling body. "Oh! Oh, Teddi, help me get back into bed! It's coming! The baby's coming!"

Teddi felt helpless to do anything but help Dora get back into bed. There was no opportunity to phone because Dora was clutching it as doggedly as she was Teddi's arm.

This, then, Teddi thought numbly, was why they called it *hard labor*. Nobody could have put more effort into it, breathing quickly and rhythmically, fingernails digging into

Teddi's arm, straining to push the infant out of her womb.

"Now!" Dora cried, and strained with all her might, finally releasing her hold on Teddi's arm and on the phone to fasten instead on the bars at the top of the bed.

Teddi had thought that the moment she could get away, she would run for help. But it was too late.

Both repelled and fascinated, she watched the tiny dark head emerge, then the entire body slid free, bringing a gushing of blood and water onto the sheets she had prepared.

At the last minute she remembered that she was supposed to catch the baby with the blanket.

He was warm and wet and messy, but suddenly the mess didn't matter. He was alive, moving between her hands, and he was the most extraordinary, wonderful thing Teddi had ever seen.

"Is he all right? Lift him up so I can see him! Make sure he cries," Dora commanded.

The infant threw out his limbs in a wild spasm and let out a squawk as Teddi folded the receiving blanket around him.

"Do I still have to hold him upside down?" Teddi asked. She was beginning to shake, unable to believe that it was all over.

"Do it just in case there's anything in his throat that needs to run out." Dora was still trying to get her breathing under control. "Here, hand him to me, and you get the scissors, there on the stand, and cut the cord."

Teddi had not thought she could do that, but she did, and finished up by tying the demanded knot.

Dora, pale and sweating and triumphant, stared at her. "I told you I could do it. Now I have to get rid of the afterbirth, while you clean him up and put him in the bassinet."

"Clean him up?" Teddi felt stupid, all thumbs, but she finally managed to fetch a basin of warm water and a cloth. The baby cried the entire time she was washing him, lying beside Dora on the stained sheets. "Now what do I do?"

"There are diapers and some little shirts in the top drawer. When he's dressed, wrap him in a clean blanket. They like to be wrapped tightly, they feel more secure that way. Then put him in the basket, turned on his side."

Teddi couldn't help being impressed with Dora's knowledge. Clearly she had studied the whole process well ahead of time. Of course that had been essential, since she'd expected to deliver the baby without medical help. *If it had been me, with no assistance except for an ignorant fourteen-year-old girl, I'd have been terrified.*

She *had* been terrified, just observing. She wasn't scared anymore, but she was shaking in reaction to what had just happened.

She dried the baby gently, put on one of the diapers that looked as if it had been intended for a doll, and then one of the miniature undershirts. He calmed down when she wrapped the clean blanket around him and picked him up.

He weighed almost nothing, Teddi thought. She had never held a creature so small. Even the puppy she'd once owned had been bigger than this. She was filled with wonder, at the birth, at the baby himself.

She almost hated to put him down in the white-painted

basket. She swallowed hard, feeling her eyes fill with tears at the miracle of it all.

"Teddi! Dora! I'm home!"

Teddi turned toward the doorway as the hall light came on.

"I'm sorry I was so late. We talked far longer than we'd intended, and it must have been midnight before I started for home. Then I had a flat tire and had to find a phone, and after that I waited practically forever for a man to come and fix it. . . ."

Mamie came to a halt on the threshold of the room. "What . . . oh, dear heaven, have . . . have you had . . ."

"A boy, just like I told you," Dora said.

"Oh, gracious, Teddi, you didn't call anyone?"

"She wouldn't let me," Teddi said, not mentioning how forcefully adamant Dora had been. "Come see, Mamie."

The wonder was not only her own, Teddi thought as she watched Mamie. Mamie's eyes filled with tears, and at the same time a smile softened her face. She reached down and picked the baby up, cradling him against her shoulder. "Oh, isn't he beautiful! He looks perfect!"

"I couldn't see anything wrong with him," Teddi said, and wondered if that were the understatement of her life. "Except maybe he's kind of red."

"That means he's healthy," Mamie assured her. "If he were pale, we'd be concerned."

Dora spoke from the bed, tired but satisfied. "Does he look like Ricky?"

Mamie lowered him from her shoulder to look into the

little round face. "Well, not yet. Give him time. He's still a bit squashed from coming into the world. Look, he's trying to suck his fist. Do you want to try to nurse him, Dora?"

"I guess so. They say that nursing makes your uterus contract faster."

Mamie carried the baby over and put him in Dora's arms, her touch lingering and tender. "I think maybe we'd better call Dr. Woods and see if he'll make a house call, dear."

"No," Dora said instantly. "It's all over, and we're both fine."

"I'm sure you are, but it can't hurt anything to play it safe. Dr. Woods delivered both of my boys, all those years ago, and while he doesn't usually make house calls anymore, I think I might be able to persuade him to make an exception in this case. Besides the possible health issues, you'll have to have someone verify information for his birth certificate. Daniel Richard Thrane."

Mamie suddenly bent over the bed and kissed Dora's forehead. "Thank you, Dora, for giving me such a beautiful grandson, such a wonderful blessing! I can't tell you how grateful I am to have something of Ricky left, when I thought I had lost everything!"

Dora guided the baby's mouth to her breast, where he nuzzled frantically for a few seconds before finding the nipple. "He is cute, isn't he?"

Mamie stood beside the bed, watching, with a joy on her countenance Teddi had thought would never be there again.

The telephone had fallen off the edge of the bed during

those last frenzied moments. Unobtrusively, Teddi picked it up. She was not part of this moment, she thought. In the hallway, she plugged the phone back in and slowly climbed the stairs. Mamie could call now if she wanted to.

Teddi couldn't remember ever having been more tired in her life.

It seemed as if eons had passed since she'd come home with Jason. His window was already dark. She opened her own window for fresh air and stood staring out, hoping he would still be awake and notice her light. She wanted to tell him about the baby.

But . . . the house next door, and her mother's old room, remained dark.

As she was drifting off to sleep, Teddi wondered again, too weary to consider it for long, who Dora had been calling from the pay phone a few hours earlier, just before she went into labor.

Chapter 7

DR. WOODS CAME and examined both the baby and Dora, and pronounced them perfectly healthy. He raised his eyebrows over the decision to have the baby at home, but other than a wry comment about medical treatment being available for everyone whether they could pay or not, he let that part of things drop.

Mamie was clearly ecstatic about Danny. She was undaunted by the washing of heaps of sheets, by a new mother who needed waiting on, by being awakened from sleep by the thin cry of a hungry infant.

Teddi felt a bit like a fifth wheel—unnoticed and unnecessary. Yet she, too, was fascinated by the tiny boy who sucked so ferociously on his fist when he was hungry, who looked so angelic in his sleep.

In the exhausted exuberance following Danny's birth, she wanted enthusiastically to tell someone about him. She was delighted, then, when on the morning after Danny arrived, her friend Callie showed up at breakfast time.

Callie had been on a trip with her grandmother to a family reunion in Kansas City. She didn't know anything about Dora or the baby. She sank onto a chair opposite Teddi and accepted a sugared doughnut while Teddi told her all that had happened in the few weeks she'd been gone.

Teddi felt closer to Callie than to any of the other girls she knew. During the months when her mother was dying, Teddi hadn't had much time for friendships. She had had to help at home, with meals and laundry and what little house-keeping got done. There hadn't been many opportunities to join the activities of the other girls in her class, and most of them seemed almost to have forgotten her. But not Callie.

Once in a while, when Callie had been offered more than one baby-sitting job for the same night, she'd recom-mended Teddi in her place. Teddi had been glad of a chance to earn a little money. One time, with the Ross kids—there were six of them—they'd shared the duties. If Teddi hadn't been tied so closely to home while her mother was so bad she'd have had more families calling *her,* she supposed. As it was, she was grateful to Callie for sharing, because there wasn't much in the way of jobs for fourteen-year-olds.

Callie lived only four doors down. They usually walked to school together, which at least gave them a chance to talk. Once in a while she had slept over with Teddi, which was fun even though they had to keep their voices low so as not to disturb Teddi's parents. Callie had been Teddi's principal support, aside from Mamie, when Stan Stuart committed suicide.

When Dora, still in her housecoat, wandered into the kitchen, Teddi was brave enough to ask, "Can Callie see the baby?"

Dora, yawning, poured herself a cup of coffee. "Sure. He's sleeping, I think."

So they tiptoed into the room that had once been Teddi's, to peer into the bassinet.

"He's so tiny!" Callie marveled. "Have you held him? I mean, except when he was first born?"

"Just that once, so far." The baby was none of her doing, of course. Yet Teddi felt a surge of pleasure and pride in Danny, almost as if he were her own family.

"He's darling," Callie murmured. "Are they going to stay here, living with you and Mamie?"

Teddi shrugged. "It looks like it. So far nobody's mentioned their going anywhere else. Mamie is so thrilled with him, she can hardly stand it. It's nice to see her smiling again."

By the time they got back to the kitchen, Dora was seated at the table, eating a doughnut, while Mamie was frying eggs. Since Mamie had eaten earlier, the eggs had to be for Dora.

"I hoped you could come over and see the new outfit Grandma bought me in Kansas City," Callie said after greeting Mamie.

"Well, if Mamie doesn't need me here, the new guy next door offered to give me a tennis lesson," Teddi said. "At ten."

Callie's eyes grew round with interest. Teddi had known they would. She had once heard another girl remark disdainfully that Callie was so predictable she was boring. But Teddi liked her that way. She enjoyed knowing that Callie would take her side in any dispute, that Callie wouldn't get into a snit over some minor issue, that Callie liked the same kinds of books and videos and music as she did.

"There's a new guy next door? Tell me about him."

So they went out on the back porch, beyond Dora's ears, and talked.

A few of the kids at school teased them about the disparity in their looks and sizes. Where Teddi was rather tall and fair, Callie was short and dark; they were as opposite as they could be. So Callie now said wistfully, "No boy has ever invited me to do anything. Do you think it's just because I'm so little I look like I'm twelve instead of fourteen? Or is there something else wrong with me?"

"It's probably mostly because they're intimidated by your brains," Teddi told her, laughing. "Mamie says boys don't appreciate brains until they get a little older."

Callie, who sat on the porch rail facing the house next door, said suddenly, "Is this Jason coming now? Wow, he's cute."

Teddi swiveled to face him, wanting to tell him about Danny, too. She felt oddly shy about it, though. She wasn't sure boys were much interested in babies.

"You ready?" Jason asked, whacking a pair of tennis rackets against his leg. He was wearing white shorts and a red knit shirt, and Teddi thought "cute" was an understatement. "I missed seeing you last night. I even decorated my new window shade for your benefit, and when I got it up you didn't bother to look over and see it."

"I was busy delivering a baby," Teddi told him after she'd introduced him to Callie. "I didn't get to bed until it was almost time to get up again."

"A baby? Dora had her baby?" And then, as the full significance of what she'd said hit him, he said, "*You* delivered it?"

"Well, sort of. Dora had the baby, and I was the only one here, so I did what I had to do. Mostly she told me, like cutting the cord and everything."

"No kidding! How come you didn't call for help?" He sounded impressed.

"I wanted to, but Dora said she couldn't afford to go to the hospital, and she wouldn't let me call 911. Um, do I need to change clothes to play?"

"Cutoffs, T-shirt, tennis shoes. You look okay to me. Let's go, and you can explain to me all this business about delivering a baby. We got the bed ready for him just in time, didn't we?"

"I'd better go," Callie interjected quickly. "Come over when you get a chance, okay?"

"This afternoon," Teddi promised. And then, to Jason, "Let me tell Mamie where I'm going." She felt a twinge of guilt as she stuck her head into the laundry room. "Jason's offered to teach me to play tennis," she said to Mamie, who was folding sheets. "Is it okay? Or would you rather I stayed here and helped?"

Mamie smoothed the top sheet on the stack. "No, go ahead. I've done all these things before, many times, even if it was a long time ago. I always wanted to know how to play tennis, but I never seemed to have a teacher and the time to try it at the same time. Oh, wait, I'll give you some cash. On your way home would you pick up a few things from the store? We have baby clothes and disposable diapers, but we hadn't gotten around to things like Baby Wipes, and Q-Tips to clean his ears, and I think maybe we ought to have a few cloth diapers. They make such good burp cloths."

"Okay," Teddi agreed. "I'll see you around lunchtime."

They went down the steps and around the house together, Jason swinging the rackets. "It must have been pretty scary, delivering a baby."

"It was. Dora said there wouldn't be anything to it, though, that women have been delivering babies with no help for hundreds of years, and she'd read up on what had to be done."

"I'm glad it was you and not me," Jason said with feeling. "I suppose Mamie's all excited to have a grandson."

"Yes. She was so devastated when Ricky died, and now it's as if her life's been given back to her."

There must have been some reservation in her voice, because Jason looked at her sharply. "Don't you want that to happen?"

"Yes," Teddi said slowly, matching her strides to his as

they headed for the park. "I'm just not sure about . . . Dora."

Jason made a sound deep in his throat. "Kind of . . . lazy, is she?"

Immediately, Teddi felt a stirring of guilt. "Well, she seems quite content to have Mamie wait on her. And me, a little bit. But of course, when she first came, she was pregnant and not feeling too well. And now she's had the baby and hasn't had time to recover. So it's probably not fair to make that kind of judgment."

Yet she *had* made it, hadn't she? There was this small but unmistakable thread of resentment running through her, though Dora really hadn't done that much to make her feel uncomfortable.

"Give her a few more weeks," Jason advised, "and see how she does. Listen, you know anything about the game of tennis?"

She shook her head, so he explained the basic rules, and Teddi willed herself to remember what he said.

They had to wait about ten minutes when they reached the park, and they watched two boys who were finishing up. Teddi knew who they were, though they were several years older than she was and, outside of exchanging greetings when they met on the street, they'd never had much to do with one another.

Still, they walked over to where Teddi and Jason were waiting, and she introduced them. They were friendly, asked Jason about his classes in the fall and his general interests, and invited him to join them in a swimming competition at the local pool.

Teddi felt him being pulled away from her, and wondered if she were becoming selfish and unrealistic. She was the first one Jason had met since his family moved in next door, and it stood to reason that he'd make other friends as soon as he met other kids. It was possible he wouldn't bother with her at all once he got acquainted with those closer to his own age. But somehow she'd hoped that she and Jason would remain friends.

She had nothing to complain about in her first tennis lesson. Jason was patient with her ineptitude and, instead of humiliating her when she didn't do it very well, he made her laugh. A sense of humor, Mamie had told her, was one of the most important characteristics a man could have as a companion.

Because she arrived home just as the mailman was coming up the walk, Teddi was the one who accepted the mail. Ordinarily she paid no attention to what he brought. The only mail she'd gotten in a long time were two postcards from Callie that came while she was in Kansas City.

Teddi didn't know why she leafed idly through the handful of envelopes, since she didn't expect anything herself. An electric bill. An ad from a local department store. A notice of some kind about a church activity. And an envelope from an insurance company. It was crumpled and dirty, as if something had happened to it in transit, even torn on one corner. The post office had stamped it DAMAGED IN HANDLING and MISSENT TO PORTLAND, OREGON.

Then her eye caught another detail, and Teddi came to a standstill at the foot of the front steps.

It had been mailed in Los Angeles on the date Ricky's plane had crashed, a date burned into Teddi's mind for all time.

A small prickle of alarm ran up her spine, though she didn't know why. She left that envelope on the top of the stack as she carried the mail into the house and handed it to Mamie.

Mamie didn't react to the envelope itself, but cut it open with the letter opener she kept on the desk just inside the dining room door.

A moment later, she gave a small gasp. "Oh, my dear God," she said, and handed the contents of the letter to Teddi before she sank into a chair. "Oh, Lord!" And she started to cry.

Chapter 8

DORA APPEARED from the living room where she'd left the TV blaring. "Is something wrong?"

"I don't know," Teddi said blankly, with an uncomprehending glance at the printed form in her hand.

Tears continued to slide down Mamie's face. "Oh, Ricky! Bless your heart, son! Bless you!"

She groped for a handkerchief and wiped at her eyes and nose.

Dora came to stand beside Teddi, taking the paper out of her unresisting hand. She frowned as she scanned it, and then suddenly cried out in understanding. "Insurance! Before he got on that plane, Ricky bought flight insurance for two hundred and fifty thousand dollars!"

"It's not that I wouldn't have welcomed Ricky's wife and child anyway," Mamie managed to say, blowing her nose. "I would have seen that you were taken care of. But oh, what a difference this will make! A quarter of a million dollars!"

Teddi swallowed. Mamie had taken her in, after some papers had been filed to allow her to consider Teddi a foster child, and there was a small sum payable for her care, so she wasn't completely a charity case. But she'd been wondering how Mamie could take on a daughter-in-law and a grandchild, and keep her, too.

She knew Mamie had a small pension, and there had been some savings when her husband died. Luckily the house was paid for, so there was no mortgage. Yet Teddi was fully aware that Mamie lived a basically frugal life, spending almost nothing on luxuries.

Teddi had traveled very little, and only once on an airplane. But she remembered overhearing a conversation between strangers at the airport regarding flight insurance. "It's so cheap to buy insurance for one trip," a wife had said to her husband. "What can it hurt?"

The couple had been laughing. "If my plane goes down, you'll be the richest widow on Fourteenth Street," the husband had pointed out.

"If we have the insurance, I *know* nothing will happen to you," the wife told him. "Buy it, and I won't worry about you. If you're worth all that money, you'll be perfectly safe, because I never got something for nothing in my whole life."

It had been a joke, a lark, when they approached the booth where the flight insurance was sold. Teddi had watched with no special interest as they made out the papers, handed over the fee, and returned to their seats opposite Teddi and her father, still joking. The husband tore off part of the form and handed it to his wife.

"There. Don't lose it. If my plane disappears or crashes during this flight, you'll need to file this as proof that I bought the insurance."

"At least with this," the young woman had said, "I wouldn't be dependent on my parents until I could get a job."

"Just don't get carried away and put a hex on my plane," the man told her, grinning. "Don't be tempted by all that wealth."

Struck by a sudden thought, Teddi blurted, "Who's the insurance made out to? I mean, who's the beneficiary?"

She knew that word because there had been a small check from insurance when her mother died. Unfortunately, the policy her father had owned had a suicide clause in it; it had not been in effect long enough to pay if he took his own life.

That was one of the many things that Teddi had found so painful. Why had he done it, when he knew that he was leaving no provision for his only daughter? How could he have cared so little for her that it hadn't mattered if Teddi were left orphaned and penniless?

The other two women were staring at her. It was Dora who recovered first and reconsulted the form.

"It's addressed to Mamie, right? Yes, she's the beneficiary."

Mamie sat up straighter. "Oh. Yes, so it says. That's odd;

you'd think he would have designated you, Dora. Especially since he knew you were pregnant. He would have wanted to provide for you and the baby."

"Force of habit, probably," Dora said. "He was used to naming his mother."

"But he never bought insurance before," Mamie said slowly.

"How do we know?" Teddi asked. "His plane never crashed before."

"No. But this copy, or one like it, would have been sent before he got on the plane, wouldn't it? That's the whole point of the notification. If he had kept the only proof of having bought insurance, it would have been lost with him." It suddenly dawned on her that Dora, as Ricky's wife, might feel hurt that her husband had named his mother to receive his insurance benefits. "I'm sure he didn't mean to cut you out, dear. Maybe he thought that if anything *did* happen, it would be better if funds were in my hands to take care of you. Since you were so close to delivering a baby."

"I'm sure that's it." Dora smiled suddenly. "It doesn't matter, does it? The wonderful thing is that he *did* buy insurance, and it will make things easier for all of us."

"The baby's crying," Teddi noticed suddenly.

Dora, engrossed in reading the terms of the insurance policy, murmured, "Would you check and see if he's wet, Teddi?"

Teddi left them figuring it all out and went back to her old bedroom, feeling strange about it. She had only moved out such a short time ago, but already the atmosphere was completely changed.

Even though a few of Teddi's possessions were still there—a few pictures, some books in the white-painted bookcase, a teddy bear left over from early childhood—Dora's belongings had taken over, along with the baby's. Her clothes were scattered around. Every flat surface was cluttered with magazines and odds and ends; and of course the crib, the bassinet, the stacks of disposable diapers, and other baby paraphernalia were everywhere, transforming the place from a teenager's bedroom to a nursery.

The baby's face was red and screwed up into a protest as his thin wail made known his discomfort. Teddi bent over the basket, looking down at him.

"What's the matter, Danny?" she asked softly. He didn't seem to be wet. She hesitated, then lifted him out of his tiny prison, cradling him against her shoulder and patting him instinctively.

Danny released a few belated sobs, then subsided into her warmth. "You're going to be all right," she whispered against his soft little head. "Your daddy bought an insurance policy, so you aren't poor anymore. Your grandma will see you're well taken care of."

She stood there for a time, rocking him back and forth, murmuring reassuring words, until he gradually relaxed and closed his eyes.

It had been so terrible, the day the news came about Ricky and the plane crash, waiting for news that his body had been found, the grief both at his loss and finally at the knowledge that, like a few others in the more than two hundred people onboard, his remains might forever rest beneath hundreds of feet of water at the bottom of the Pacific Ocean.

After the two recent funerals of her own parents, Teddi hadn't looked forward to another burial, this time of the young man who had lived next door. But it was obvious that a body to bury might have been helpful to Mamie. She needed that for closure on the tragedy. She had been so grief-stricken at first that Teddi had almost feared for her sanity, though that period hadn't lasted long.

The lethargy into which Mamie had then sunk had been almost as bad. Neighbors and church friends brought in food for which Mamie had no appetite. Guiltily, Teddi had sampled casseroles and cakes and pies, then wrapped them in foil and put them in the freezer.

Though Teddi seldom mentioned her own losses, and she saw a similar restraint in Mamie, it had been a period of deep mourning for them both.

And then Dora had arrived, and now Danny was here, warm and soft and helpless in Teddi's arms.

Maybe, Teddi thought hopefully, the sadness would eventually be put aside, and life . . . a good life . . . would go on.

Danny was sound asleep now, but Teddi was reluctant to put him down.

She stood for some time, rocking him to and fro, enjoying the feel of the peach fuzz hair against her cheek. No doubt Mamie remembered when it had been Ricky she held in this way, and no doubt, too, there would be tears when she held Danny, instead.

But please, God, let them be healing tears. Otherwise,

nobody could bear the pain, Teddi thought.

She wasn't even aware that her own cheeks were wet as she cradled Dora's baby, cuddling him while he slept.

The summer days fell into a pattern.

Most mornings, Teddi had a tennis lesson at the park. At first she was so incompetent that she was tempted to stop trying, but Jason was patient and quietly encouraging.

"Nobody starts out like a pro," he told her. "I'm probably not even the best teacher. But I can help you learn the basic stuff. And it's fun, and good exercise."

Sometimes they had to wait to get a court, and they would stand watching the others, often talking between themselves. She always enjoyed talking to Jason.

To her surprise she found one day that she could tell him a little about her father.

"I guess we were never very close," she said. "He was always so busy with his work, and in the evenings he liked to tinker around with his woodworking in the garage. A few times I tried to go out and talk to him, but he made me feel like a nuisance, so I didn't do it very often. It was funny. He and Mom could talk for hours together, and before she got so sick she and I talked a lot. But Daddy and I never did seem to have much in common."

"Sometimes I can't talk to my dad, either," Jason said. "If I really want to persuade him to let me do something or have something, I talk to Mom first. *She* can talk him around better than I can."

Teddi nodded. "My mom did, too, before she was sick.

Then it was like she just wasn't up to it anymore. I didn't want to bother her when she didn't feel well. And the sicker she got, the more Daddy worried about her and ignored me. Except when he reminded me that we needed clean clothes or something cooked, he hardly paid any attention to me at all. Some days I felt as if he wasn't even aware that I was in the house."

Jason sighed. "Yeah. That would be rough. Dad notices me, all right. He's always telling me to pick something up, put something away, get my act together. And *not* to borrow his yellow shirt, or eat the last of the roast because he wants it for his sandwich the next day. I guess you'd have been grateful for even that much."

"I would have," Teddi affirmed. "I could sort of understand what he was going through, because we knew Mom was dying. For a while we hoped maybe the chemo would work, but for several months before the end we knew there wasn't going to be a miracle. We were going to lose her."

Jason watched her face with sympathetic eyes. "It hit him pretty hard."

"Yes. Me, too, but he never noticed about me because he was hurting so bad himself. He was devastated when she finally died. The doctor had to give him some pills to get through the day of the funeral. Nobody asked if *I* needed anything. And then he came home and holed up in his den and didn't talk to me. It was awful, but I figured he'd get over it, the way other people do."

"Only he didn't," Jason said softly. "Instead, he committed suicide." He sighed. "A kid likes to think his parents are stronger and wiser than he is," Jason murmured. "Sometimes they aren't, I guess."

It has been strangely comforting to confide in Jason. And later, when they got a court and played until both of them were sweating and tired, Teddi thought it was one of the best days she'd had since it all happened.

Other days there were kids sitting on the sideline benches, watching, which made Teddi nervous. It was one thing to be awkward while learning the game, another to be under close scrutiny when she flubbed a shot. Once in a while someone shouted, "Good one!" For the most part the only negative comment from the spectators was an occasional collective groan when she missed the ball entirely.

Gradually, though, Teddi got better. And as she grew slightly in self-confidence, she realized something: The spectators were mainly teenage girls, and they were watching Jason more than they were watching her.

Once, three girls from that group met her in the grocery store and stopped in front of her. "Are you going with that new boy, Jason?" one of them asked.

Teddi knew the girls by name; they lived in the neighborhood. They were all juniors in high school.

"No," Teddi said. "He lives next door, is all, and he offered to teach me to play."

One of the other girls rolled her eyes appreciatively. "I wish he'd offer to give *me* lessons," she said.

Other than during the tennis lessons, however, Teddi didn't see much of Jason, except when they called across to each other before they went to bed at night. Even so, she felt an odd sort of comfort knowing he was there, not very far away, in the room that had been her mother's. And every time she saw the cartoonlike character he'd sketched in colored markers, grinning at her from the new/used shade on his window, she had to laugh. It was good to laugh again.

The tennis lessons and Jason's presence were welcome diversions. There were other changes at home that were less gratifying, though some were pleasant.

Teddi sometimes heard Danny crying at night, but it didn't usually bother her much. Dora was generally good with him, so they didn't have to listen to the baby for long before he was fed. And in the daytime Teddi enjoyed hanging over the bassinet when Dora moved it out of the bedroom. He was so tiny, yet so perfect, with fingers that would already curl around a larger finger offered to him. He didn't do much but sleep, stretch, yawn, and eat; yet in his own way he was fascinating.

Teddi wasn't alone in being enthralled by the baby. Mamie was only too eager to hold him, to rock him, to carry him around on her shoulder, singing or talking to him. There was no question that Mamie's spirit had been revived by having a grandson in the house. Teddi was glad to see it; she had felt so helpless, after Ricky's death, at her inability to comfort Mamie.

Along with the good changes, there were, of course, those other changes in the household routine that were a source of discomfort to Teddi.

She didn't mind that there were more dishes to do and added cooking chores. It wasn't much more work to prepare food for three rather than for two people. But a thin layer of resentment had begun to build within her about some of Dora's habits. Dora *did* have to awaken early to feed the baby, after which she went back to bed, not to arise until midmorning. Then she shuffled into the kitchen in her housecoat and slippers, hours after Mamie and Teddi had cleared away their breakfast dishes.

More often than not, Mamie fixed eggs or hot cereal or pancakes for Dora. If left to her own devices, Dora usually settled for coffee and toast, or cold cereal.

"A baby needs more nutrition than that," Mamie would say. "Why don't I scramble you some eggs?" Teddi had the feeling that if she hadn't been having a tennis lesson, she might have been pressed into that cooking chore when Mamie was busy elsewhere. And not only the cooking, but the washing up, because Dora just left her dishes in the sink, not even rinsing them.

And there was the matter of Dora's tastes. Dora didn't like salads much, though Mamie loved them. She preferred cooked peas or carrots. So cooked vegetables appeared more often on the menu. She didn't care for brown bread, either, and though Mamie urged her to try it because it would be healthier for the baby, both white and brown bread eventually appeared on the table. Dora liked a brand of peanut butter that had sweetening in it, though Mamie had always purchased one made only of peanuts and salt. Dora didn't like any kind of jam except for strawberry. Dora drank soft drinks, can after can, ignoring Mamie's gentle urgings to drink more milk.

"Never could stand milk," Dora said, shaking her head. "The taste of it gags me."

So Mamie got a bottle of calcium capsules and left them on the kitchen table, reminding her daughter-in-law daily that both she and the baby needed calcium if Dora was not going to drink milk.

Where Mamie and Teddi liked fresh vegetables either raw or cooked in the steamer, Dora found them too firm. Left to her own devices, she would have cooked everything from green beans to broccoli until it disintegrated into mush.

Mamie tried hard not to nag about anything. She made it a point to cook what Dora said she liked, even when it often meant cooking it longer or differently from what she and Teddi were used to. Occasionally, as when they had a mess of fresh fried fish, brought over by a friend from church, she cooked something altogether separate for Dora, who objected to picking out bones.

"I seem to be getting my strength back very slowly," Dora remarked at one point. "But I suppose it's normal. In the old days women used to stay in bed for a couple of weeks after giving birth, before they moved around at all." This from a woman who had insisted on having her baby alone at home because women once gave birth anywhere they were—even in the fields.

Some days Teddi thought Dora might as well have stayed in bed. She took frequent naps and spent a lot of time stretched out on her bed or the couch, reading magazines or watching TV.

The TV was another sore point. Because it was always

Teddi and Mamie who cleaned up in the kitchen at night, Dora would already be arranged on the couch watching TV whenever they reached the living room.

Mamie only had a couple of programs that she watched regularly. Teddi enjoyed those, plus a few more that she watched when there was nothing else to do. But with Dora already propped on pillows on the sofa, remote control in hand, nobody else got a chance to choose programs.

"Mamie usually watches that news show," Teddi said once, only to be told, "Oh, really? Would you mind, just this once, if I finished watching this? It's really interesting."

And Mamie smiled and said, certainly, she'd get the news out of the paper tomorrow.

Teddi seethed, unable to turn the situation around.

She might have gotten downright resentful if Dora had been disagreeable to her. But except for lapses like eating the last piece of pie that Teddi had been saving for her snack, for which Dora apologized, and monopolizing the couch and the TV, it was hard to blame Dora. She was a new-comer to the household and did not yet know the customs here. Teddi had been the same only a few months before when she moved in.

"She'll get used to things, and fit in," Mamie said sooth-ingly, "when she's feeling fully recovered."

It made Teddi only too aware that she, too, had had to adjust to a new life. So how could she begrudge Dora a sim-ilar period?

"I nearly talked you to death when I first came," Teddi remarked to Mamie as they stood together, folding clothes from the dryer one afternoon. "I just had to talk about my mom and dad, even when I knew it was hard on you, Mamie. But Dora hardly ever mentions Ricky."

Mamie nodded, folding a tiny undershirt to add to the stack already on the table. "People react in different ways to grief. When my husband died, and then Ricky, I needed to talk about them, too. But Dora is a different kind of person. She keeps things in. Maybe, in time, it will be easier for her to talk, to ventilate her sorrow. When that time comes, we'll listen. Until then, we'll let her grieve silently."

Teddi was glad that her friend Callie was home again. They spent hours together, at either Mamie's house or Callie's, talking, listening to music, or watching videos. Sometimes they simply sat together in the same room, reading and eating apples or cookies. When Teddi wanted to talk, Callie was there. When Teddi felt like being quiet, Callie was willing to share the silence.

One evening at supper Dora asked, "How long do you think it will take to get the insurance money?"

"I don't know. I filled out the forms they sent me. Ordinarily insurance isn't payable unless there is proof of death. But in this case there were forty-two people whose bodies were never recovered, and never will be. Yet the computer records show that they were all on that plane that went down. The woman I talked to seemed to think it wouldn't be very long before the claims were paid. There's no real hurry. We know that it will be paid. We'll set up a trust fund for Danny, for his education. That would be one of the first things Ricky would want for his son."

"A trust fund. That will mean the money can't be used for anything else, won't it?"

"Yes. I've talked to a lawyer, and that's what he recommended. There will still be plenty left to ensure that you're both taken care of while Danny's growing up."

"And maybe put a new roof on the house?" Teddi asked suddenly. "Didn't you say you were worried about the roof lasting another winter?"

"Yes. It leaked a little bit during that last heavy rain in the spring. I had that fixed, but the man said the whole roof would need replacing before long."

Dora wasn't interested in leaky roofs. "Do you have a will, Mamie? Ricky didn't have one; he didn't think he needed one because he was only twenty-six and he didn't expect to die so soon. But I guess everybody needs to think about such things, no matter how young they are."

"Yes. The lawyer mentioned that, too. I'll be going in next week to talk about a will. I don't have all that much, except for the insurance, but even this house will have to be disposed of. I'd always thought it would be sold, and the profits divided between my sons. It's only fair, now, that Danny should have Ricky's share."

"Well, his daddy won't be around to look after him. I'm glad that at least he won't grow up in poverty," Dora said.

My dad didn't worry about me living in poverty, Teddi thought. *He didn't think about me at all. Only himself, that he missed Mom so much.*

It had hurt badly when her mother died. And it had hurt almost as much when she lost her father. But most of all it hurt to know that Stan Stuart hadn't cared enough about his daughter to make any arrangements for her care and her life after both her parents were gone. Would she ever get over resenting that? Or would she carry the burden of it forever?

That night, after she'd put on her pajamas and turned out the light, Teddi raised the shade and looked out on the house where she had once been part of a happy family.

The opposite window was dark. Either Jason wasn't home or had not yet decided to go to bed. Teddi left her own window open, with the shade up enough to let the air flow through beneath it.

It was a very warm night, and the attic room was stifling. Teddi turned and walked across the room to open the second window as well, hoping for a cross breeze.

This window looked out on the street, which at this time of night was deserted. The streetlight provided illumination to the immediate area, except where trees and shrubs cast heavy shadows.

As soon as she'd opened the window, a cooler draft promised relief from the heat. She stood there for a moment, welcoming the change in temperature.

The click of a latch below held her a little longer. Curious, Teddi waited for enlightenment.

There were soft footsteps on the porch, and then a dark-clothed figure went down the steps and out toward the sidewalk.

Dora? Where was she going at this time of night?

Yes, as the woman passed beneath the streetlight, it was unmistakably Dora. Hurrying, as if time were important.

Going for a walk? Heaven knew Dora didn't get any exercise during the day, but this seemed an odd time for a stroll, even a hurried one.

Well, it wasn't any of her business, Teddi told herself. There had been a few times when she'd wanted a walk at night herself, just to think and sort things out. Probably Dora had plenty of things to want to sort out.

Teddi was tired, but for some reason she didn't go to sleep the way she usually did. After a period of twisting and turning, trying to get comfortable, she decided she was hungry. Since she wasn't sleeping anyway, she thought she might as well go down to get a sandwich or something.

She didn't bother with a robe or slippers. In her bare feet, she padded downstairs and felt her way toward the kitchen. There she turned on a light, knowing it wouldn't bother anyone even if Dora or Mamie had a bedroom door open.

She found baloney and mustard and constructed a sandwich, adding to it a can of cold pop from Dora's supply. She had turned out the light and reached the foot of the stairs when she heard the front door opening.

Teddi hesitated, expecting Dora to turn on a light, but nothing happened. The door latched with a barely audible sound. She couldn't even hear the girl walking toward her, though she sensed it.

Dora's bedroom door opened almost—but not quite—soundlessly, then was relatched behind her.

No thread of light appeared under the door. After a few moments, Teddi turned and made her way upstairs with her snack, wondering uneasily what that had all been about.

Chapter 9

WHEN JASON HAD NOT arrived by a little
after ten the next morning, Teddi decided to save a few
minutes by walking over to meet him. Heidi and Annie
were sitting on the front steps, reading.

Annie looked up reluctantly. "Jason's in the garage, fixing a tire on my bike," she announced. "Just go find him,
why don't you."

For a moment Teddi hesitated. Her mouth had suddenly gone dry. Slowly, her knuckles turning white on the
handle of the racket Jason had lent her for the duration of
the tennis lessons, she forced herself to move.

She got as far as the open garage door and felt totally
unable to proceed any further. She stood there, staring

into the dim interior, heart hammering.

Jason was kneeling, doing something with a tire on the floor. When her shadow fell across him, he looked up.

"Hi. I'll only be another minute or two. Come on in."

Teddi scarcely recognized her own voice. "I . . . I can't."

"Can't?" Jason's hands went still. "What do you mean, you *can't?*"

Feeling suffocated, Teddi stepped backward. "I'm sorry. I . . . can't go in there."

For a matter of seconds, Jason registered only confusion. And then his eyes narrowed. "Is this where it happened? Where your dad committed suicide? Here in the garage?"

Teddi gulped audibly, beyond speaking.

Jason came swiftly to his feet, abandoning the bike. He emerged into the sunshine, one hand with a firm grip on her arm, propelling her away from the house. Behind him, the opening to the garage was a yawning black hole.

He swore softly, inoffensively. "Breathe deep. Sit down on the bench for a minute."

Knees close to buckling, Teddi obeyed. Jason sank onto the seat, too, keeping his hand on her arm. "Did you find him?"

Teddi nodded, closing her eyes against the sight of the open garage, yet continuing to see it behind her closed lids. She heard her own voice, as if coming from a long way off. "Sorry. This was the first time . . . since they took him away."

"I should have asked you before, but I thought Charlie was just shooting off his mouth when he told me he was surprised we bought the house after your dad died here. He's kind of an irritating slob. I think he likes to say things that upset people. You feeling better now?"

Teddi opened her eyes. "Yes. Except for Mamie and Callie, I . . . I haven't talked to anybody about it. He . . . closed up the garage and piped the exhaust fumes into the car. . . ."

Jason's hands gripped her upper arms as he swore again. "And he left it to you to find him and deal with the mess. Look, Teddi, we don't have to have a tennis lesson this morning. You want to skip it for today?"

Teddi made an effort to pull herself together. "No. No, I feel like I need to move, to do something physical."

Jason's hand slid down one arm and clasped her hand, drawing her up with him.

"Come on. Let me get my racket and we'll go. Annie," he called out to his sister, "I'll finish with the bike when I get back, okay?"

They walked slowly and, at first, silently toward the park. Finally Teddi cleared her throat. "Would your folks have . . . bought the house, if they'd known?"

"Oh, sure, they love the house. And they're not superstitious or anything like that. If nobody ever bought a place where somebody had died, three quarters of the houses in the whole country would be vacant, wouldn't they? It must hurt a lot, knowing your dad did that without thinking you'd be the one to find him."

Her throat was tight and painful. "It does. There was a suicide clause in his insurance, which meant there wasn't even anything to take care of me. If it hadn't been for Mamie, who came in and fought for me to get to take me as a foster child, I don't know what would have happened to me."

"Mamie seems like a real nice lady. She's had her own troubles; she knows what they feel like. I'm glad she took you in. And now Dora and her baby."

Teddi stirred a little, inwardly, thinking about Dora. "It was a real shock when Dora showed up on the front steps, looking ready to deliver that baby. I wondered if that would mean I'd have to . . . go somewhere else, find a different foster home. It's different, with Dora and the baby there. Sometimes I feel really uncomfortable about them, for some reason, but Mamie's so happy with a grandson. How can I begrudge her that, without being a . . . a selfish pig?"

"It's only natural to think about your own predicament. I guess anybody would. But you're getting a little bit used to Dora, aren't you?"

"Yes." Teddi remembered a few of the oddities, though. "I don't know what to think about her walking a few blocks to make a call, when there's a phone right there in the house. And last night, after everybody'd gone to bed . . . Dora went out for a while. I've never seen her walk for exercise or anything like that, not in the daytime. Of course Danny's there, but we'd watch Danny while she was gone if she wanted to walk. She didn't ask either of us last night. . . . Mamie had gone to bed and was reading with the radio on when Dora left, but she wouldn't have turned off her light and gone to sleep if she'd known the baby was alone across the hall . . . and I thought it was . . . strange."

"What seems strange to me is that Mamie's son would marry some girl and never tell his mom, especially after he knew they were expecting a baby."

"That seems funny to me, too," Teddi admitted. "And about the insurance, too."

"What about the insurance?" Jason wanted to know as they approached the tennis courts.

"He bought it at the airport, before he got on that plane. And he made it out to Mamie as the beneficiary, not to his wife. Wouldn't you think he'd have made it out to Dora?"

"Yeah," Jason agreed. "Hmm. Hey, looks like those kids are just leaving the court. Let's claim it before anybody else gets here."

It felt good to get hot and sweaty, running around the court, smashing the ball as hard as she could. By the time they walked home, Teddi was almost back to normal.

As they parted, Jason said, "Thanks for introducing me to those other guys. They've asked me to do things with them a couple of times. A movie, bowling. It's kind of hard to get acquainted when it's too early to meet kids in school. Did I tell you that I've got a part-time job, starting next Saturday? At Harada's Grocery, putting up stock. It'll be a little spending money, and maybe I'll get more hours by fall, if one of their clerks quits then to go away to school. He's talking about it."

"That's great," Teddi said, forcing enthusiasm. If he worked Saturdays, that would end her tennis lessons on weekends. "Well, I'll see you later," she told him, and walked into the house.

Everything was quiet except for the muted sounds of the TV. Dora was in her customary position, sprawled on the couch, watching a soap opera. Mamie was nowhere in sight.

Mamie despised soap operas. "I've had enough trouble in my own life," she had once observed, "to want to steep myself in anyone else's miseries."

Yet Mamie was the one who always came to the rescue when someone was in trouble. It wasn't only Teddi and Dora; it was anyone in the neighborhood or the church who needed help. Mamie was always making a pot of soup or a casserole to carry to someone, and attending a funeral or sitting with an acquaintance to talk out a problem or a sorrow.

Teddi didn't interrupt Dora's TV. She walked past Dora's open bedroom door, then Mamie's, to use the bathroom to wash up. On her way back out, intending to head for the kitchen to see what might be interesting for lunch, she heard the baby begin to whimper.

Teddi hesitated. He wasn't really raising an outcry yet, the way he would if he were hungry. It was probably safe to leave him alone until he did.

On the other hand, Dora often was the last one to hear him when she was watching TV. It covered Danny's small sounds.

Teddi enjoyed looking at the baby. She hadn't yet gotten used to admiring the tiny, perfect fingers and toes, and the little round pink face as it yawned or howled or relaxed in sleep.

The door to the room *was* open. She didn't feel that she was invading Dora's privacy by stepping over the threshold, bending over the bassinet.

Danny's eyes were squeezed shut, but he was squirming restlessly.

"What's the matter, you have a gas bubble?" Teddi asked very softly. "You want someone to pat you on the back?"

She picked him up, ever so carefully supporting his head, loving the feel of the downy hair under her hand. Over her shoulder he went, with a cloth diaper under his face so that if he spit up it wouldn't go all over her.

She patted for a few moments, murmuring soothing words, and eventually Danny rewarded her with a gentle *burp*.

"That all of it? Okay, back to bed, then," Teddi told him, and eased him once more into the bassinet.

Dora had rearranged the furniture when they brought in the crib and the big basket on legs. Teddi had forgotten that there was a small square table just inside the door, behind her, until she bumped into it and knocked something off.

It was Dora's purse, an inexpensive sling-type black bag, and in falling it spewed out its contents across the floor.

Teddi bit back an exclamation, glancing apprehensively to the doorway, afraid Dora might show up and resent finding her here.

Quickly, before that should happen, Teddi dropped to her knees and began to gather up the contents to return to the purse. It was a simple one, with only one compartment, and Dora didn't carry much in it. Lipstick, a few coins, some Kleenex, a compact, a comb, a ballpoint pen, half a package of gum.

Teddi scooped them all up, then returned the purse to the table.

She was halfway out the door into the hallway when she stopped, suddenly struck by the thought that something was missing.

She turned, glancing toward the living room where voices were raised in some sort of confrontation on the TV. Then she stepped quickly back into Dora's room and opened the purse up wide to verify the impression she'd had.

There was no wallet. No I.D. of any kind. No driver's license, no Social Security card, no credit cards. No personal correspondence, no snapshots.

Wasn't that kind of odd? Teddi had often enough been sent to get something out of her mom's purse, and even a few times from Mamie's, to know that most women carried more than Dora did.

Teddi's own purse, sparsely filled as it was, had a Junior High Student Body I.D. card and a wallet with a few pictures, even though it didn't often have much money in it.

How did anyone get along with no personal identification? Even teenagers carried *something* to show who they were. How come Dora didn't?

In the kitchen, she saw a note on the table from Mamie.

Salad in the fridge. Fresh fruit in the bowl. I'm over at Mrs. Hall's, helping with her laundry. She burned her hand and can't do much today. If the paperboy comes to collect, take the money out of the jar.

The jar had once held mayonnaise, but now it was where Mamie dropped her change. It sat inside the cupboard next to the sink. Teddi glanced at it as she got down a glass for milk, noting that it had a few bills in it this time, too, including a twenty clearly visible among the ones.

She carried her lunch out onto the back porch to eat and read a few chapters in the latest library book.

It was several hours later when she saw the paperboy coming and got down the jar to pay him.

"Thanks," the boy said, and handed over the current paper.

It wasn't until Teddi reached up to put the money jar back on the shelf that she noticed the twenty-dollar bill was missing.

She paused, then reached in to pull out the currency, laying it out on the counter. Three one-dollar bills and assorted change. But there was no twenty.

Teddi replaced the bills in the jar, feeling uneasy. Mamie hadn't taken the twenty; she was just coming in the front door right now.

Danny set up an outcry, and Teddi moved to the hallway in time to see her pick up her grandson and cuddle him. "I think he wants his mama," Mamie said, patting him as she carried him toward the living room. "That sounds like a hunger cry to me."

"He's always hungry," Dora agreed, accepting him. "This time you get to eat in the living room, kiddo. I want to see the end of this program."

Mamie smiled a little. "I need to make a phone call. If you don't mind, I'll turn down the TV a little bit."

"Sure," Dora said. "I guess it would be better if I had a set in my room so I could watch whatever I want when you want to watch something else out here, wouldn't it? Do you suppose that insurance check would stretch to something like that? Another TV set?"

"We'll talk about it," Mamie said. "Of course the money won't be here for weeks, probably. Maybe even months. Insurance companies don't work very quickly."

Mamie went into her room and closed the door, stretching the phone cord out behind her. Dora was unbuttoning her blouse to feed the baby.

Teddi hesitated as heat swept over her in a guilty flood at what she was thinking.

Instead of going upstairs, as she'd intended, she slipped boldly into Dora's room. Her heart was pounding, and she didn't know what she'd use for an excuse if she were caught, but she moved swiftly to the purse still standing open on the table.

One glimpse inside was enough.

There was a single twenty-dollar bill in plain sight, and some quarters Teddi didn't think had been there before.

There was a pain in Teddi's chest. It hurt to breathe. She pressed the heel of her hand over the pain and walked quickly out of the room, scarcely aware of anything except that Mamie's new daughter-in-law apparently was a thief.

Chapter 10

IT WAS THE MOST uncomfortable afternoon Teddi had ever spent in Mamie's house.

She went over and over it in her mind, like an equation in algebra, trying to make it come out with a different answer.

Somehow, Dora must not be a thief. Yet the evidence was there, so clear that Teddi could reach no other conclusion.

She was positive there had been a twenty-dollar bill in the mayonnaise jar when she was fixing her lunch. It had been gone a few hours later when she paid the paperboy.

Virtually the entire contents of Dora's purse had spilled out when Teddi knocked it off the table. It had held perhaps a dollar or two's worth of coins. There had been no bills.

Then after the money had disappeared from the jar, a twenty had magically, horribly, appeared in Dora's purse.

Mamie had been gone all afternoon. She could not have taken the money or given it to Dora. Teddi even managed to verify that Mamie had not once run back home for anything. She had had no chance to do anything with the money.

While Teddi was mulling this over, further potential complications occurred to her.

Mamie seldom put anything more than silver and single-dollar bills into the jar. Not once since Teddi had been living there had she seen the jar holding a twenty, until today.

Dora wouldn't know that.

Sooner or later, probably the next time she went to drop change into the jar, Mamie would notice that it no longer held a twenty-dollar bill.

What if she thought that Teddi, rather than Dora, was the culprit?

A wave of icy sickness swept over her as she realized Mamie might think *she* had pilfered the money.

How could she prove otherwise?

To explain how she knew that the money had not been in Dora's purse earlier in the day, and how she knew it was there later, she would have to admit looking, not once but twice. Teddi's face grew hot and she felt guilty, even though she had never touched that twenty-dollar bill. There was no way to explain without *seeming* guilty.

Who would believe the truth?

If she went to Mamie right now and told her what she believed, wouldn't Dora deny any knowledge of the money, or of how it came to be in her possession? Dora might even accuse Teddi of planting the evidence on her, in a fit of jealousy.

And if it came to a choice, believing Dora or believing Teddi, how would Mamie choose?

A shudder of something close to anguish ran through Teddi's body, just thinking about it. Dora was family, while *she* was only a neighbor kid Mamie had taken in out of the goodness of her heart.

Oh, please God, don't let Mamie think I've repaid her kindness with this kind of treachery!

She had prayed when she opened the door into the garage and seen her father slumped in the front seat of the car, too. *Oh, no! Please God, don't let him be dead, too!*

But that prayer had not been answered. What chance did this one have?

Mamie did not seem to notice that anything was wrong with her. She was talking about Mrs. Hall's burned hand and how she'd urged her to see a doctor, so they'd gone together to have it taken care of.

"She won't be able to get it wet for at least a few days," Mamie related, checking the refrigerator crisper for the makings of a salad. "Teddi, honey, would you put this together in that green glass bowl?" She had put lettuce, tomato, green onions, and a jar of marinated artichoke hearts on the counter. "Maybe throw in the rest of those ripe olives, too. There isn't time to bake an omelette now, so I guess we'll just have hamburgers."

Teddi moved automatically, getting out a paring knife and the cutting board, scarcely aware of what her hands were doing. When she realized they were shaking, she thought for sure Mamie would realize something was wrong with her.

But Mamie was busy with her own thoughts. She chatted on about Mrs. Hall and a friend they'd met in the doctor's office, one who had foot problems.

"Alice Thorgild has a new grandchild, too. Of course we had to exchange grandchildren stories. Danny is too young to have generated very many yet, but oh, what a difference it makes to know that he will! I remember so many cute, funny things Ricky and Ned did when they were little, and I'd thought all of those things were gone forever for me. And now look! So much to look forward to!"

Teddi couldn't come up with a response to that. In fact, her throat felt as if it were closing; she had trouble breathing.

Sooner or later Mamie would know about the missing money. She was going to reach a conclusion, rightly or wrongly, about what had happened to it. It would destroy her trust in one or the other of them, Teddi or Dora.

The smell of onions was strong as Mamie put the hamburger patties in the frying pan. Usually Teddi loved the aroma of hamburger and onions; today, it was making her sick, and she wondered how she'd ever manage to get through supper, through an evening of waiting for the bomb to fall, when Mamie learned that money was missing.

Teddi's parents had always told her it was better to confess before being caught for a misdoing. But here she hadn't done anything wrong, except look in Dora's purse, which had seemed justified under the circumstances. There was no way she could confess the truth as she saw it without accusing Dora.

Dora had finished feeding the baby and put him back in his basket; she came into the kitchen as Mamie was dishing up the hamburgers and patties made from leftover mashed potatoes.

"Is there anything you want me to do?" Dora offered.

"No, I think everything's ready. Teddi, do you want to say grace tonight?"

Ordinarily they took turns. Dora, shortly after her arrival, had declined to take a turn, telling them, "I wouldn't know what to say."

Tonight it was almost more than Teddi could do to think straight, but she had to make an effort. She fell back on a simple little verse her mother had taught her when she was no more than a toddler.

"'For food and drink and happy days, accept our gratitude and praise; in serving others, Lord, may we repay in part our debt to thee.'"

She sat opposite Dora, which was torture. It was hard to look at her, yet at the same time it seemed important to study her perfectly ordinary, pretty face.

Dora ate and drank, responding to questions Mamie put to her. She laughed at the story of Ricky losing a four-foot-long garter snake in the laundry room for two weeks, so that Mamie was reluctant to enter the room. She clearly enjoyed hearing about the time Mamie had been cooling four pumpkin pies intended for a church bake sale. Ricky, age two and a half, had reached up to the table over his head and taken a good handful of filling in each hand and eaten it with great relish.

"So you couldn't sell the pies," Dora observed.

"So we had to buy them ourselves," Mamie said. "Oh, I can't wait until Danny gets up to those tricks!"

Teddi's pain grew worse. What would Mamie do if Teddi told her about the money and Mamie believed her? Would she throw Dora out, giving up this new but quickly loved grandchild?

Of course the more likely scenario would be that Mamie would believe Dora, and that it would be Teddi who would go. Or, not much better, be allowed to stay but be lectured about stealing. How could she stand to be tolerated but be under suspicion from that time on? It would be even more painful than if she were actually guilty of the crime.

How could she even consider depriving Mamie of that baby? Ricky's son, all she had left or would ever have of her younger son?

When her mother had become too ill to serve as her confidante and confessor anymore, it was to Mamie that Teddi had come in moments of stress. Mamie had advised her on school problems, on how to deal with a difficult teacher, on how to avoid getting involved in a feud between two warring factions of girls.

Mamie had always taken a commonsense attitude toward these problems. Her advice had usually worked out fairly well. But she couldn't go to Mamie with this, not without hurting her irrevocably.

If it hadn't been for the baby, Teddi wouldn't have had much compunction about telling on Dora, even knowing that she herself would be at risk as soon as she did. Mamie would be hurt knowing either of the girls in her house had violated her trust, but Danny made it a different matter altogether. The moment Mamie had seen Danny for the first time and held him in her arms, she had loved him with all her heart.

Teddi couldn't wait to escape from Dora's presence, but Dora seemed to make that impossible.

"Why don't I clear up tonight?" she asked. It was the first time she had ever made such an offer. "That is, if you wouldn't mind watching Danny for me, Mamie? Maybe rocking him if he's fussy?"

"I'd like nothing better," Mamie declared. "Teddi can tell you where things go."

Teddi's mouth went dry. How could she be alone with Dora?

She was rescued by Callie, who called on the phone. "Can you come over and help me decide between two outfits? We bought both of them, but Mom says I can only have one, so I have to take the other one back tomorrow. Please, Teddi?"

"I'll check with Mamie. I'm supposed to be helping Dora put things away," Teddi said, eager to flee the house.

"Oh, I'll figure it out," Dora assured her, to Teddi's surprise and relief. "Go ahead, if it's all right with Mamie."

All the way over to Callie's, Teddi debated whether or not to confide in her friend. Maybe Callie would have some insight into how to handle the situation.

They picked the top and skirt that Callie would keep, and Teddi drew in a deep breath. "Listen. I need some advice, but you have to promise not to tell anyone else, okay?"

Callie listened to the whole story, looking more disturbed at each revelation. "Maybe Mamie won't notice the money is gone. I mean, she throws change in there all the time, and I doubt if she keeps very close track of it."

"Not the silver, or the ones. But how could she forget she dropped a twenty in there? Sooner or later she's going to remember. And it could only be me or Dora who took it. If I'm going to say anything to Mamie with any chance she'll believe me, it has to be right away. The longer I wait, the more phony it will sound that I noticed, that I knew and didn't say anything until somebody suspected me. Mamie will think I lied when I got caught."

Callie wanted to help, but she had no answer, either.

Teddi walked home through the twilight, worrying, uncertain what to do.

She made no decision. Mamie and Dora were in the living room, watching television, turned down lower than Dora usually played it. It was a sitcom of the type that Teddi and Mamie had never watched; one of those silly, slapstick things with occasional raunchy bits of dialogue. It didn't take a brain surgeon to figure out who had picked that show, Teddi thought wryly.

During a commercial, which Dora muted, Mamie cleared her throat and said, "I'd like to watch the ten o'clock news tonight. I'm going to bed a bit early, I think."

"Oh," Dora said flatly. It was clear that she already had something else picked out, but it was, after all, Mamie's TV. "It would sure be handy if I had my own set, wouldn't it?"

Still, Teddi held back, unable to bring up the matter of the twenty-dollar bill that had been removed from the jar. The news only partially held her interest. Political news, a bad accident on I-5 involving two cars and a semi, an update on a little girl who was recovering from a bone marrow transplant, a judge's verdict that a little boy who had been adopted over a year ago should now be returned to his birth mother. The sorrow of the adoptive parents twisted the knife in Teddi's heart. Would it be any better for Mamie if she lost Danny?

Dora, who had been reclining on the couch, sat up abruptly about ten minutes into the news. "I think I'm going to find a book and read in bed for a while."

So the evening was ending, and Teddi still had not said anything. The situation seemed more dismal by the moment.

Mamie was heading for bed, and Teddi accepted her hug good night at the foot of the stairs before going up. She couldn't yell across to the house next door about the quandary she was in, but she was hoping Jason would be there so that they could talk for a few minutes.

However, his window remained stubbornly dark.

Teddi went to bed, falling into a troubled sleep that cul-
minated in a dream of an infant wailing and herself being
pursued by an unseen enemy, then falling, falling. . . .

She jerked awake, disoriented, realizing it had been
only a dream. She turned her head to check the clock beside
her bed. Twenty past midnight.

She punched her pillow, then turned it over to find a
cooler spot. And then she heard a continuation of her
dream: a baby crying.

For a few seconds Teddi waited for Dora to get up and
tend to Danny. But nothing happened. The thin whimpering went on and on, until at last Teddi got out of bed, feeling annoyed. Didn't Dora realize that Mamie needed her
sleep, that the baby should be fed or whatever he needed, so
that he didn't wake up Mamie?

Mamie's door was closed, however, when Teddi went
downstairs. She must be sleeping soundly. Probably, Teddi
had to admit, she wouldn't have heard the baby herself if
she hadn't been awakened by the bad dream.

The door to Dora's bedroom was also closed. Danny's
fussing was barely audible to Teddi as she stood in the hallway, listening.

"Come on, Dora, get up and tend to him," she muttered
under her breath.

The whimpering became a full cry.

After a moment's hesitation, Teddi rapped lightly on the
door and said, "Dora?"

There was no response.

A second rapping brought no results, either.

WILLO DAVIS ROBERTS

Teddi glanced across the hall at Mamie's door, expecting her to emerge at any moment.

If she knocked any harder to rouse Dora, she'd undoubtedly disturb Mamie, too.

On impulse, Teddi twisted the knob and opened the door to peer into Dora's room.

Now the crying was loud enough to be heard more clearly. She quietly closed the door and turned on a small lamp, illuminating the bed on the far side.

It was empty. The covers were turned back, as if Dora had been sleeping in it, but now she was gone.

"Dora?" Teddi looked around, but there was nowhere to hide unless she was in the closet, which wasn't likely. The bathroom? No, that door was open, and the bathroom was dark.

Teddi drew a deep breath and crossed to the bassinet, where the baby, red faced and upset, continued to emit those unhappy sounds.

"What's the matter, buddy?" Teddi leaned over him, feeling the light blanket and then the sleeper Danny wore. Everything was soaking wet. Not only that, it was *cold* soaking wet.

"How long you been lying here like that?" Teddi asked softly. "Hey, now, I'm here, don't cry."

She picked him up out of the sopping basket and looked around for something to change him into. There was nowhere to lay him except in the crib, which he had not so far used, so she put him down there, with a waterproof pad beneath him.

110

He had stopped crying the moment she picked him up, but started again as soon as she put him down.

"Okay, give me a chance to find some clean clothes. Ah, there they are." Still in the laundry basket sitting on the dresser, neatly folded by Mamie as they came out of the dryer. Teddi found a clean sleeper and undershirt, then a disposable diaper from the package at one end of the crib.

His little body felt clammy as she stripped him of the soggy garments. How many times had he wet the diaper for it to have leaked so much? she wondered. The things were supposed to be practically leak-proof, according to the TV ads.

Once he was re-dressed and wrapped in a clean receiving blanket, she held him against her shoulder, where he quickly calmed down.

Not until he had fallen asleep again did she put him into the bassinet in fresh sheets and a blanket. How much time had passed? Twenty minutes, anyway.

Where was Dora?

She turned out the light, reclosed the door on the sleeping baby, and went looking.

It was a small house. It didn't take long to determine that Dora was not in it.

And the front door had been left unlocked.

Where was Dora? she continued to wonder uneasily as she climbed back upstairs to her own bed.

Chapter 11

GOING BACK TO BED did not mean going back to sleep.

Teddi lay in the semidarkness, thinking.

She had been devastated when her mother died, even though they had known that it was going to happen. And then her father had committed suicide, and in a place where he must have known that *she* would be the one to find him.

Had he even thought about it? About her?

"What kind of father does that to his kid?" she had cried out in a paroxysm of pain and grief. "How could he do that to me? I'll never forgive him."

And Mamie had held her and let her cry, and tried to answer. "His own anguish was so great that at least at that moment he was incapable of thinking of anything else," she told Teddi. "Losing your mother was probably the most awful thing that had ever happened to him. I suspect he was simply incapable of going on without her. It wasn't that he didn't love you, Teddi. I know he loved you. I'm sure he cared. But he was hurting so much that he felt he had to find a way to end it, and I doubt if he considered anything else. Not even you.

"We're all human, honey," Mamie had told her gently. "Even when we're trying to do our best, we fail other people sometimes. We don't mean to. We just don't always have the strength to do what we ought to do."

Teddi had recognized the truth of that. A month after her father's death she had sat beside Mamie in church and listened to a sermon on the necessity of forgiving those who have wronged us. Not once, not even seven times, but seventy times seven times.

Which meant, Mamie had explained when they talked about it later, indefinitely.

She remembered how she had asked, her face stony, "So I'm to just forgive my father for abandoning me the way he did, letting me find him dead in our own garage, sitting in the front seat of the car? It's not that easy."

"No, it's not easy. But it's the only way you'll find peace of mind, Teddi. Your anger and resentment isn't hurting *him,* you know. It's only hurting *you.* It's . . ." Mamie had groped for the right words. "It's like a sort of acid, poured over your soul. Until you can forgive him, it will continue to hurt you. Forgiving causes the acid to begin to be washed away, so it doesn't keep on eating away at you."

They hadn't talked about it since, but though Teddi felt she had sincerely tried to forgive her father, she knew she hadn't really accomplished it.

Yet she had come, and quickly, to trust Mamie. Mamie was only a neighbor, a friend, yet she had stepped in to embrace a homeless orphan, to offer her the security that she needed so badly.

And now that security was threatened—by a young woman neither she nor Mamie had even heard of a few short weeks ago.

Dora. She had arrived on their doorstep, moved in, taken over their lives. Disrupted the peace that had begun to heal Teddi's heart.

They'd never heard of her, knew nothing of her. But look at Dora now.

How did they even know she *was* Ricky's widow?

The thought came with the suddenness of a hammer blow. Teddi's breath caught in her chest.

She lay very still, consciously expelling the air caught in her lungs, deliberately inhaling another breath, forcing herself to calm down.

How did they know?

Only because Dora said so. Oh, she'd shown Mamie a marriage certificate. But an official document could be faked, couldn't it? People used computers for all kinds of things like that, including printing out counterfeit money that looked real enough for the forger to get away with it for a while. There'd been a case like that in the paper not long ago. All Dora would have needed was a copy of a genuine certificate to copy and the use of a computer to do it on.

Mamie apparently had been convinced by the marriage certificate. But there was no other I.D. of any kind. Nothing to signify that Dora was Mrs. Richard Thrane, or what her name had been before they got married. Ricky, peculiarly enough if Dora's story was true, had not told his mother about her. He had, only moments before boarding the airplane on which he had died, made out an insurance policy *to his mother,* not the wife who was pregnant with his child.

Ricky had been too much older than Teddi for them to have been close buddies, but he had been a casual friend. He had waved when he saw her as he was coming and going, and once when she'd crashed on her bike and had a bloody knee, he'd had her sit on the front steps while he got a washcloth and a Band-Aid.

She'd watched from next door when he'd brought his friends home with him. Teddi had been fascinated by the tall, athletic young men with bottomless appetites, judging by their overheard conversations, and by the pretty, mostly athletic young women who occasionally accompanied them. Funny that Ricky would marry a couch potato like Dora, when he had enjoyed so many sports and more energetic activities.

And now, staring up at the ceiling that was barely visible through the night, Teddi wondered again, *How did they know that Dora was really Ricky's widow?* Only by a single piece of paper that could have been produced on any modern computer.

Of course some men didn't marry the same type of woman they'd dated beforehand. She supposed even a jock didn't necessarily stay a jock when he grew up and took on a responsible job and wanted a family.

But the lack of I.D. took on increased significance as Teddi pondered it. Now that she considered it carefully, it seemed incredible to her that they'd accepted Dora's claim of relationship with so little hard evidence.

Was it only wishful thinking to imagine that Dora, for some inexplicable reason, might be an impostor?

Unable to lie still any longer while such thoughts swirled in her head, Teddi got up and walked to the window to look down on the silent street with its alternately lighted and shadowed areas.

The crazy idea, once implanted in her head, was ready to grow by leaps and bounds. She was wide awake now, not sleepy in the slightest.

Why would Dora pretend to be Ricky's widow if she were not?

She had come here within days of giving birth, and without much in the way of funds. So the obvious answer was money.

Yet if she knew anything about Mamie, she must have been aware that Mamie was not wealthy. She had this small, ordinary house and a small pension that enabled her to live comfortably without having to hold a job, but hardly in luxury.

Except that now they knew there was a large insurance policy. Only how could Dora have known about that if Ricky had not told her about it? And if Ricky had told her, why wouldn't he have made her the beneficiary rather than his mother?

No, Teddi thought after a few moments of reflection,

Dora could hardly have known about the insurance.

The answer still had to be money, didn't it? Maybe not a lot of money, but certainly Mamie's modest house and income were proving to be adequate for a girl who needed a place to go at a time when she couldn't look after herself very well.

A refuge in the time of storm. The phrase came to her, unbidden. Wasn't there a hymn about that? Of course. They'd sung it not long ago at church, only it was "A Shelter in the Time of Storm." Shelter, refuge. A place one sought to wait out a difficult time.

Like giving birth to a baby. Giving birth without medical attention, insisting she could not go to a hospital, no matter what.

Teddi couldn't imagine approaching childbirth the way Dora had. She couldn't even have been certain that an ignorant fourteen-year-old would be around to assist her; she had planned to have Danny entirely on her own.

Teddi remembered how Dora had jerked the telephone free from the wall, then hung on to *her* so that she couldn't possibly plug it back in and summon help.

Along with the lack of driver's license, Social Security card, or other I.D., there had been another item lacking in Dora's purse. There was no insurance card. Dora had said she could not afford to go to the hospital, which was undoubtedly true. But Dr. Woods had said that if they had taken Dora to the hospital, she would have been taken care of. Mamie had mentioned getting her on Aid to Dependent Children. Would that agency have demanded identification beyond what might be a bogus marriage certificate? Dora had been quick to state that Ricky never would have wanted her to accept welfare. Yet she seemed to have no hesitation at accepting whatever Mamie could provide, and was even hinting about wanting other material things.

So what other reason would there have been for staying away from a hospital at a time when most people would have considered it essential?

Did the lack of proof that she'd been married to Ricky have anything to do with it? Because whether she had money or insurance or not, Dora surely would have been expected to provide something to prove who she was.

Might there be other things Dora was not prepared to reveal to anyone? Had she been afraid that the stress and pain of delivering her baby might let her slip and divulge some truth that she did not want known?

She was getting far afield here, Teddi knew, yet the path her thoughts were pursuing was too compelling to reject. In the distance, where insects fluttered around a streetlight, something moved, but she was too engrossed in her own speculations to pay much attention.

The more she thought about Dora, the more Teddi was convinced there was something very peculiar about her. *Was* it merely wishful thinking to believe there was a serious problem here, beyond the fact that Dora appeared to be a thief? No, Teddi decided.

She brought the room's only chair to sit beside the window, leaning her elbows on the sill, welcoming the faint cooling breeze as it stirred the hair around her face. It was time she thought things through very seriously.

It was Mamie the airline had notified when Ricky's plane went down. Mamie who was told that his body had not been recovered and that it probably never would be.

Why Ricky's mother, rather than his wife?

Why did Dora not even have a snapshot of her supposed husband?

Why didn't Dora talk about her life with Ricky? She was willing, even eager, to listen to Mamie's tales about Ricky's life before marriage. But Teddi couldn't recall a single instance of a specific anecdote from Dora about her husband.

There were occasional general comments. They'd liked a certain little Italian restaurant in San Diego. They'd enjoyed a movie, a walk, a book. (Though Teddi couldn't imagine Ricky reading any of the books she'd seen Dora read so far.)

Below her on the street, a figure emerged from shadows, and Teddi's pulse suddenly quickened.

It was Dora. She was sure it was Dora, and she waited until the streetlight directly overhead made it a certainty.

For a moment Teddi was tempted to go downstairs, to confront the woman, right now at nearly two o'clock in the morning. She imagined turning on the light just as Dora stepped inside the front hall, and saying, "Danny cried and cried, so I came down and changed him. His bed was soaked. How long did you leave him alone? Where have you been?"

Would that awaken Mamie? Was she, Teddi, ready to confront Dora, in front of Mamie?

Her mouth went dry, thinking about it.

No, not tonight, Teddi decided. But maybe soon.

In the meantime there must be things she could do to

119

find out about Dora's background. If there was evidence anywhere that Dora was not what she claimed to be, Teddi had to have it before she challenged her.

If Dora had made up the whole story she'd told, she was about as bold and brazen as anyone Teddi could imagine.

And therefore, if challenged, she would surely fight back. So before Teddi faced that, she would need as much information as possible.

In the morning, as she came downstairs, the doorbell rang. Since she was the closest, Teddi answered it.

It was a delivery man with a very large cardboard carton, its contents named on the package: a color TV.

"Package for Thrane," he said, consulting the slip he had gripped in one hand, then taking the paper between his teeth so he could maneuver the carton.

"Oh, it's here already!" Dora said, opening her door and sounding pleased. "Can you carry it into my room, please?" She grinned at Teddi. "Wasn't it nice of Mamie to let me get it now, without waiting for the insurance money?"

Teddi felt her jaw sagging and snapped her mouth shut. When had Dora talked Mamie into that?

But that wasn't the biggest shock of the morning.

When Teddi was putting away her breakfast dishes after they'd been washed, her eyes were drawn at once to the mayonnaise jar where Mamie kept her change.

Teddi's heart seemed to stop beating. For there was a twenty-dollar bill, right on top of the smaller bills and the change on the bottom of the jar.

Chapter 12

"YOU WEREN'T THINKING about tennis," Jason told her as they left the court. It wasn't an accusation, simply a statement of fact.

"No," Teddi admitted. "I wasn't." For a few seconds she hesitated, reluctant to put her inner turmoil into words. Since her mother's death, Callie and Mamie were the only ones with whom she had shared her worries and fears.

But this situation was too much for her. She was scared, and she was angry, and though she was still determined to get to the bottom of the circumstances surrounding Dora's arrival here, she was not a detective. She didn't know what to do, or how to do it. She made the plunge.

"Would you mind listening for a few minutes, and then giving me your opinion?"

Jason grinned. "Sure. Nobody in my family ever solicits my opinion on anything beyond which video we should watch, and then they usually overrule me. There's an empty bench over there, and nobody's close by. Let's sit down."

So she told him. The whole thing, including all the wild things she had thought last night as she sat alone in the dark, waiting for Dora to return to the house.

"Am I crazy?" she asked at the end of the recital, to which Jason had listened without asking more than an occasional question. "Could it be possible that Dora's an imposter, not Ricky's wife at all? Could anybody come here this way, lying about such a thing?"

Jason's face was thoughtful and concerned. "Well, I don't think you're crazy. When you lay it all out that way, it's pretty overwhelming evidence. The why is probably money. She hopes to gain from taking advantage of Mamie."

"But Mamie has so little. Just a small pension, and now the insurance. And nobody knew about the insurance before Dora came."

"Maybe Dora did, somehow."

It made her feel a little better already, knowing that he didn't think she was irrational.

"How could she? Until the notice showed up in the mail, Mamie and I didn't even know about it."

"Maybe she was there when Ricky bought it. At one of those booths in the airport, right? Where you can walk up on the spur of the moment and make out a simple form that says if you don't make it through your flight, the insurance company will pay your family?"

Teddi nodded, eager for some logic, for a possible explanation that hadn't occurred to her. "How would she know, though?"

"Maybe she was working in the booth and had carbon copies of the insurance policy, something like that, that gave her his name, and Mamie's, and their addresses. Or maybe she was just sitting next to him in the airport waiting room and overheard him mention the policy." He gained enthusiasm as he let his imagination run free. "Maybe he talked to her about it, the way people do sometimes with strangers in a place like that. Nobody expected that plane to crash into the ocean, but it did, only a matter of minutes after takeoff. If she had talked to him, she'd remember him, it happened such a short time later. And she decided to take advantage of it."

"And made up all this elaborate hoax right on the spur of the moment?" Teddi asked, incredulous.

"Maybe. Maybe right at first all she did was keep track of who he was and where he was from. And then when they started recovering bodies, and they couldn't find them all, and his name was on the list of the ones still missing . . . well, by that time she'd had a few days to think about it. And she obviously needed help, didn't she? She was pregnant and broke. Desperate, probably. And there was this guy she knew about, who wasn't ever coming home to call her a liar. Maybe she was desperate enough to try to rip Mamie off, even if she didn't know about the insurance money. Mamie could have been no more than a person to take her in and pay the bills until she could handle a baby and take care of them both herself. But I'm betting she knew about the insurance. Which probably means she was there at the airport just before he took off."

Teddi felt light-headed, she was so grateful that he was taking her seriously, not ridiculing her convictions regarding Dora.

She had told him about the twenty-dollar bill that had been in the mayonnaise jar, then missing, only to show up in Dora's purse, and then suddenly reappearing in the jar.

"Does that make any sense to you?" she demanded.

Jason chewed on his lower lip. It was gratifying that he was giving her his full attention. "Maybe. Maybe she wanted *you* to be accused of taking it. To screw up your relationship with Mamie. She apparently didn't know you were part of the picture, living with her supposed mother-in-law. You may have been an unpleasant surprise, one that complicated what she was trying to do."

"That could have happened, all right. Only why put it back?"

"Maybe it had nothing to do with you. Maybe she just needed the money—you said her purse was practically empty—and she took it for . . . something, whatever she had to do, or get . . . and then because she didn't want any suspicion to fall on *her,* she put it back."

"But if she still had it, how could she have used the money?"

Jason shrugged, watching a young mother approaching them with two small children. "I haven't figured that out yet.

To make one of those mysterious phone calls, the way she did before? What could she have been doing so late at night, except making phone calls or meeting someone? She was on foot, so she couldn't have gone far out of the neighborhood."

"She says she has no family, no friends to turn to," Teddi remembered.

"But she's in contact with somebody. Have you thought that if Ricky's not that baby's father, someone else must be?"

She hadn't gotten that far. "You think she has an . . . an accomplice? A man, Danny's father, maybe?"

Jason drew in a deep breath. "This is going to take some analysis, and we'd have a better handle on it if we wrote it all down. All the things, even the little ones, that don't fit into the story Dora tells about being Ricky's wife. Let's go to my house and put it all on paper. Of course there's a possibility that she *was* married to Ricky, and it's just that she's the type to sponge off Mamie if she can get away with it. And there's another thing. Have you thought about the baby? Mamie's crazy about him, right? If Dora *wasn't* married to Ricky, Danny's not Mamie's grandson."

Teddi's voice was small. "I know. It makes me cry to think about it. But I can't let it slide, can I? Let Dora take advantage of Mamie if she is a fake?"

"No," Jason agreed soberly, though there was an excited sparkle in his eyes at the thought of the adventure that might lie ahead. "You can't. *We* can't." He got up off the bench and reached for her hand to pull her up. "Let's go work on it."

It was the first time she'd been in the house since her father's death except for the time she'd spent clearing out her personal belongings to take to Mamie's. The furniture had all been sold to pay some of the debts.

There were changes that made the house seem alien, yet there were also plenty of reminders of the time when it had been her home. The furniture was different, of course, and the draperies were new.

There was a runner in the front hallway, a patterned rug with a floral pattern. There were unfamiliar pictures on the walls, and through an open doorway she saw that they'd repainted the kitchen so that it was now a sunny yellow instead of the pale green Teddi had grown up with.

She had not formally met Jason's mother before, and she liked her, or she would have if she'd been able to spend any time thinking about it.

"We've got to run some stuff off on the computer," Jason told his mom before they climbed the stairs.

Doors were open off the upper hall, and she saw that in her old bedroom, now home to a ten-year-old and a seven-year-old, her pale blue walls had been papered in a pink rosebud pattern.

It was Jason's room that was most disturbing, however, the room where her mother had spent her last months.

Here, too, the furniture was different. It was a relief to find a single bed, a desk, a couple of chairs, and posters for rock groups and a Save the Eagles campaign.

But the carpet was the familiar blue she remembered, and there was a slightly faded spot on the wall where Gloria Stuart had kept a painting of Jesus.

Nobody had put anything else over that area, and Teddi

wondered what had happened to the picture. She wished she had it. She probably could have taken it if she'd thought of it when she gathered things out of her own room. Now it was probably gone forever, disposed of along with all the other household furnishings.

Yet it was a tremendous comfort to have confided in Jason, and to know he'd be helping her work it out.

"Okay," Jason said, sitting down before the computer and switching it on. "Let's first list what Dora's said about being married to Ricky. And then all the things that make you think she might be lying about that."

Teddi stood at his shoulder, staring at the screen where the damning evidence grew as Jason typed. She tried to divorce herself from her surroundings, to forget that her mother had died here in this room, to think only about Dora and Danny and Mamie, and her own future.

The thing that had struck her almost immediately, Teddi told Jason, was that Dora related nothing personal about Ricky.

"After my mom died, and then my dad, I kept remembering things, you know, like how they'd laughed—way back when they still *did* laugh—and what they'd liked to eat, and how they looked. The way they did things, the things they liked. But Dora hardly mentions Ricky. Mamie thinks it's because it's too painful to remember, but I keep wondering more and more if it is because . . ." She hesitated, then blurted out what seemed such a terrible suspicion. "Because she never even knew Ricky."

"And she picked your brains for details about him,"

Jason said, fingers moving on the keyboard.

He finished up with three full pages of questionable points, then punched the keys to make them print out.

He made three copies, one for her, one for himself, and one to save for future reference.

Teddi held the pages as if they might burn her fingers. When she raised her eyes from the print, her voice was tremulous. "It . . . it certainly seems like more than a bunch of stupid wild ideas when it's all printed out like this, doesn't it? So what can we do about it? How can we find out the truth?"

Jason switched off the monitor and then the printer and swiveled around in his chair to face her.

"We're going to become spies, or detectives, if that sounds better. We're going to snoop into everything we can find about our friend Dora. If she's an imposter, we're going to expose her."

Teddi swallowed. How, she wondered despairingly, could their investigations spare Mamie any further grief?

Yet her voice was very nearly steady when she replied. "All right," she said. "How do we start?"

"We watch her every movement, and the next time she goes out on one of those midnight excursions," Jason said with satisfaction, "I'm going to follow her and see where she goes, or who she meets."

For long seconds they stared into each other's faces, and Teddi's heart was pounding as if she'd just climbed a long, steep hill.

"Okay," she agreed softly. "Let's do it."

Chapter 13

TEDDI FELT AS IF she were walking a tightrope.

What would Dora do if she knew she was under suspicion? How determined was she to succeed in bilking Mamie of everything she had?

How would Mamie feel about the plan Teddi and Jason were putting into effect? Would she be outraged at the idea that they wanted to discredit the daughter-in-law and grandson she had only just found? At the very least, whether they were right or wrong about Dora, Mamie would be terribly hurt.

Teddi watched Mamie as she went about her routine tasks, in the house and out in the garden, seeing a contentment that had not been there since the news had come about Ricky's death.

Every time Mamie looked at Danny, or held him, there was a smile that only too clearly bespoke how important this child was to her.

Dora, engrossed in her new TV, luckily, didn't seem to notice the way Teddi watched her. At dinner, though, sitting across the table, her expression seemed to sharpen at something she saw in Teddi's face.

Teddi tried—unsuccessfully, she feared—to smile offhandedly. Inwardly, she was in a turmoil, praying that no one could really read her countenance. Fortunately, that was the moment Jason chose to tap on the back door. Teddi quickly pushed back her chair and excused herself, joining Jason on the back porch rather than inviting him in.

"It may not prove anything," he said in a low voice, "because we don't know for sure that Dora and Ricky were supposed to have been married in San Diego, but they *weren't.*"

Teddi stared at him. "What do you mean?"

"I mean I called my uncle Jim, who lives in Escondido—you know, not far from San Diego—who's a lawyer, and my cousin Jenny, who works as his secretary. She investigated it and just called me back. Nobody named Richard Thrane married anybody named Dora anything in San Diego County over the past two years. I didn't figure she needed to look back any further than that, because Ricky hadn't been down there that long."

"So either they got married somewhere else," Teddi said

slowly, "or they weren't married at all."

"Right. Of course the fact that she says they lived in San Diego wouldn't have to mean they were married there, but if they were really short of money, wouldn't it be most likely they'd get married close to home, where it would be cheaper? And"—Jason paused for effect, though she was paying close attention, anyway—"there is no telephone listing anywhere in the county for Richard Thrane. Was his home address on that form he filled out for the insurance?"

"I don't remember. I wonder what Mamie did with the form after she wrote to the insurance company?"

"See if you can find it. He must have had to put an address on it. If we had that, we might be able to find out more about him. About whether he was married or not."

Finding the notification Mamie had received about the insurance Ricky bought proved to be quite easy. Teddi had been afraid Mamie had put it into her safe-deposit box at the bank, but she had not.

It lay in the corner of the top drawer in the desk, along with a few unpaid bills.

Teddi glanced around guiltily, but Mamie was out in the laundry room, and Dora was with her blaring television.

The form held both an address and a telephone number.

Teddi copied them and ran next door with the information.

Mrs. Temple let her in with a smile. "Jason's up in his room, fooling around with the computer, I think."

He turned to face her when she tapped on his door frame, and took the paper she handed him.

"Yes!" Jason said triumphantly. "Let's call this number and see what we can find out."

That plan, however, proved disappointing. Though the phone rang and rang on the other end, nobody answered.

"Well," Jason said, hanging up, "whoever's phone it is, it hasn't been disconnected. I'll try it again later. Has Dora been sneaking out of the house every night?"

"I don't know. I've only caught her a couple of times. And they were just by accident. Am I going to have to sit up all night and watch for her to leave?" It was a dismaying prospect, going without sleep, but there must be a way to trap Dora if she was the imposter they believed she was.

"Can you cover until, say, two A.M.? Then I'll take over until dawn," Jason offered.

"What'll I do if I see her leaving?" Teddi asked nervously. "Will I have to follow her?" It was a scary prospect. "What if she meets an accomplice?"

"I'll get my Boy Scout whistle for you, and we'll both leave our bedroom windows open. Give me a toot on the whistle, and I'll come running. I'll keep my clothes on, even my shoes, so it'll only take a few minutes to get on her trail."

It was the best plan they could come up with. Teddi figured Dora wouldn't leave, if she were going to, until Mamie had gone to bed and was asleep. That had been the pattern so far. So it ought to be safe to take a nap earlier in the evening, to be sure to be awake during the critical period.

A little later, back at Mamie's, she took a book and made a remark about reading in bed for a while. When she headed up the stairs, it was a little after nine o'clock. But once in her room, either napping or reading proved impossible. She was too tense.

She had Jason's Boy Scout whistle on a cord around her neck, which should have been reassuring. But what if he didn't hear it? What if he'd gone to the bathroom, or downstairs for something to eat? What would she do then?

To be ready for anything, she put on a pair of dark jeans and a black shirt—it was missing a couple of buttons, but she didn't expect anyone to see it, anyway—and dark tennis shoes.

She was as prepared as she could get.

The minutes on her digital clock changed with maddening slowness. Her inability to relax made her chest ache, and she drew a deep breath, and then another, trying to calm down.

Her conviction that Ricky and Dora had not been married to each other was stronger than ever. Surely Ricky would never have married a girl like Dora. It hadn't been a lapse of memory when he designated Mamie as his beneficiary, and Dora was no more than an opportunist who had seen a chance to insinuate herself into Mamie's household for her own gain.

And if that was the case, then what? To lose Danny, so soon after Ricky had vanished from her life, would desolate Mamie. She was already making such plans for the baby. She was planning a trust fund for his education, and she was forever spotting something that would be appropriate for a little boy: a red wagon, a tricycle, a swing set for the backyard.

There was no way this story could have a happy ending, Teddi thought wistfully. Unless by some miracle Dora *had* been Ricky's wife, and Danny really *was* Mamie's grandson. In which case, Teddi herself would probably be eliminated from the household before long, of her own volition if they didn't ask her to leave.

She didn't think she could spent the next few years in the same house with Dora. Even if she had put the money back in the jar, if she had simply borrowed and returned it, Dora had not asked to take it. Teddi was sure of that. Which meant that Dora would never be someone you could trust. Nor would Dora be likely to tolerate the presence of someone else in the household for long.

A surreptitious sound brought her into a sitting position.

From below there was canned laughter on Dora's new TV. But this had been a different kind of sound.

After a moment it came again, from outside. Through the open window at the front of the house.

Teddi reached out and turned off the reading light, throwing the room into near-darkness. Silently, she slid off the bed and crossed to the other window. Jason's room was completely black; was he sleeping in preparation for his own watch? They hadn't figured on anything happening this early, but might not Dora have used the TV for cover and slipped out of the house now through a window?

Teddi leaned as close to the screen as she could get and lifted the whistle to her mouth to give the signal: two short blasts.

There was no visible response from next door, but of course Teddi hadn't expected there would be. She hurried back to the street-side window to listen carefully again.

That first sound, whatever it was, was not repeated. She had almost given up and retreated when she heard the rapping.

Not on the front door below; she was pretty sure of that. On a window, maybe?

Teddi wished there were no screen, or that it were easily removed, for she wanted to lean out, to listen. She wished Dora would turn off the TV, for though it wasn't loud from up here, it was enough to cover small noises outside.

And then there was another sound that allowed the TV to get louder, but Teddi recognized it. The window in Dora's room slid up, sticking enough so that Teddi heard her curse, then screeching as it moved upward.

She couldn't see what was directly beneath her own window. The house was in the light from the street except right up against the building, and there was no way to twist her head to see into those shadows.

Someone was out there. Dora had opened the window to him. And Teddi heard the hissed reaction.

"You idiot! You'll blow everything!" Dora was furious.

Teddi couldn't make out the whispered response, only that it was a male voice. When Dora spoke again, she, too, had lowered her voice, so that the words were frustratingly unintelligible.

What should she do? Teddi wondered frantically. Blow the whistle again for Jason, in case he hadn't heard her first alarm? That seemed like a good idea, but then what? Go downstairs?

She put both plans into action, glad her rubber soles made her progress silent.

Dora's door was closed, so it was safe to go past it. Mamie was in the living room, listening to music and reading, her back to the doorway.

Through the house, then, to the back door, twisting the lock, sliding out into the darkness of the back porch.

A glance toward Jason's house revealed no sign of movement outside. Was he already watching the unknown visitor, or was she out here by herself?

Her heart was hammering, so that all she could hear was the blood in her own ears. Teddi paused, trying to adjust to the dimness, willing her own breathing to calm down.

Around the back of the house, then the far corner, then . . . she stopped, one hand unconsciously pressed against her chest.

There was a bulky figure beside the house and, from this close, though she still couldn't make out all the words, Teddi was sure they were quarreling in low, angry voices.

She strained to hear, catching an occasional emphatic word, mostly profanity on the part of the man. Then she thought he said, "Be there!" and Dora retorted with another burst of profanity.

The window slammed shut, and after a few seconds, the man turned and moved rapidly toward the street.

He was leaving, Teddi thought in a panic. What was she supposed to do? Where was Jason?

Wildly her gaze searched the shrubbery, the shadows under the trees, but there was no sign of Jason.

Where was he?

Already the man was striding toward the corner half a block away.

It wasn't enough to learn what they could about Dora. This man, whoever he was, was mixed up in this whole thing. It was essential to find out who he was, and what he was up to.

Teddi drew a deep, painful breath, and decided: There was only one thing to do. She'd have to try to follow him.

Chapter 14

TEDDI HAD TAKEN only a few steps when an arm reached out of the shrubbery and grabbed her.

She hardly had time to gasp when Jason said urgently in her ear, "Where are you going?"

"He was here, Dora's accomplice. He headed off that way on foot. I thought I'd better follow him. *Where were you?* I thought you were going to come as soon as I blew the whistle!"

"I'll explain later. I'll follow the guy. That's him at the corner, isn't it? You stay here and keep an eye on Dora."

He let go of her arm and was gone before she could protest.

Teddi stared after him, her pulse still racing. What

could Jason do if the man realized he was being followed? Was Dora's accomplice likely to be violent?

There wasn't much she could do about it now. Though if Jason didn't come back soon with an explanation, would she have to call the police? She didn't know what she'd tell them, or what information she had that would enable them to rescue him if he'd gotten into trouble.

She was trembling as she let herself back into the darkened kitchen. What a mess it all was, and now she'd dragged Jason into it, too. His folks would kill her if anything happened to him.

Dora's TV was still playing, and so was Mamie's music. This was too small a house to hold two simultaneous sources of sound, Teddi thought wearily. Well, maybe it would soon be over, this farce of Dora being Ricky's widow. But would things ever get back to normal, as she and Mamie had known it before Dora came? She didn't really see how they could.

Her eyes were stinging as she moved toward the lighted part of the house.

Mamie wasn't reading. She was sitting with a big photograph album on her lap, looking at the pictures. She looked up and saw Teddi and smiled.

She held a loose snapshot in her hand. "Isn't it funny? You think you'll remember some things forever, but you don't. After a while you forget. Ricky and Ned looked so much alike at the same ages that if I hadn't written on the backs of their pictures to identify them, I wouldn't be sure now which of them it is."

And suddenly the idea was there, fully formed, in Teddi's mind. It startled her so much that for a moment she was unable to speak.

Beside her, Dora's door opened and she emerged and headed for the bathroom.

Obviously she hadn't expected Teddi to be standing there, for she jumped and swerved to keep from walking into her. But she didn't pass before Teddi saw that she'd been crying.

Somehow she hadn't expected tears. It made Teddi feel funny in a way she couldn't have explained.

Mamie got up from her chair, setting the album aside, retaining only the single snapshot. She came into the hallway to join Teddi, saying, "Sometimes I can figure it out from the background, something else in the picture. I think this one is of Ricky, because he was three the year I grew the dahlias that took first place at the county fair. See how big they were?"

Water flushed in the bathroom, and after a moment Dora came out. She murmured, "Excuse me," and would have walked past them to return to her own room if Teddi hadn't spoken.

"Mamie's found another picture of Ricky when he was little. Don't you think Danny looks a bit like him?" Her mouth was dry as she told the lie, but it had the desired effect. Dora stopped, automatically looking at the snapshot in Mamie's extended hand.

Teddi swallowed hard and tried to sound natural. "He was so cute, wasn't he? He was such a good-looking guy, I always thought. It was a shame he got so badly scarred in that accident last year."

She caught Mamie's startled expression, but Mamie didn't say anything. Dora's mouth sagged open. "Scarred . . ." she echoed faintly.

"He was lucky to find a girl like you," Teddi persisted, "who didn't care about the scars on his face."

Dora licked her lips uncertainly. "Uh . . . yeah, I guess."

"They didn't matter to you, did they?" Teddi said insistently.

Dora drew in a shallow breath, and her head moved slowly from side to side. "No. No, they didn't."

There was a perceptible silence. Relief, welcome yet strangely painful, swept through Teddi's body. She shifted her gaze to Mamie, to see how she was taking this.

As she'd more or less expected, there were tears forming in Mamie's eyes. But she wasn't shocked enough to be falling apart, only deeply saddened. She looked directly into Dora's face, and her voice was oddly compassionate.

"You never even met my son Ricky, did you, Dora?"

Consternation swept over Dora's countenance. She put one hand to her throat and made a choking sound.

"I think," Mamie said, with more control than Teddi felt, "that we'd all better sit down. We have some talking to do. Maybe it would help to have some cocoa. Let's go out in the kitchen. Teddi, will you get down the mugs, and I'll do the hot chocolate."

Dora sank onto a chair, her face chalky. "How did I give myself away?"

Teddi set out the thick mugs, overcome by thankfulness that Mamie hadn't fallen apart. She didn't know what she would have done in that circumstance. She herself was feeling incredibly weak in the knees.

"You accepted the idea of the scarring," Teddi said.

"Was Ricky's face badly scarred?" Dora was bewildered, taken off balance.

"No," Teddi told her. "Ned was the one in the accident. He went through a windshield. He's been having plastic surgery for it. But when Mamie said how much the boys looked alike, it occurred to me that if you were an imposter, you wouldn't know whether Ricky was scarred or not. Unless you were the one who sold him the insurance policy, so you saw him then."

Dora reminded Teddi of a balloon with a slow leak. She was perceptibly deflating before their eyes. "No. You're right, I never met Ricky. It was Roger who sold him the insurance policy."

"Who's Roger?" Mamie asked, adjusting the heat under the milk she'd poured into a saucepan. "Danny's father?"

"My husband," Dora admitted in a small voice. "He worked in the insurance booth. He wasn't very busy right then, and he and Ricky talked. The plane went down so soon afterward, and Roger said wouldn't it be funny if any of the people who were killed were ones who'd bought insurance from him. Someone like Ricky, who hadn't seen his family for quite a while, someone single. And then when he checked on the list of survivors, and Ricky wasn't on it. . . ." Her voice trailed off, and she swallowed.

"Roger saw an opportunity for fraud," Mamie said. Mamie didn't sound angry, exactly, though there was now an edge to her voice. "He thought maybe if you could convince Ricky's mother that you'd been married to him, you could get your hands on that insurance money. And maybe more, if I had anything else. He knew I'd be excited . . . any mother would be . . . to think I had a grandchild coming. So you showed up and claimed to be Ricky's wife."

"I didn't really want to do it," Dora said forlornly. "But it was true, we needed money, and Roger said it would be easy." She gave a bitter laugh that held no humor. "Easy! Having the baby all by myself because I didn't dare go into a hospital with no identification and no insurance except under the wrong name! He said I couldn't take a chance on talking too much if they gave me anything for pain and I didn't keep my head clear, so I had to have the baby at home."

Mamie spooned cocoa mix into each of the mugs, then poured the milk into them. When Dora made no move to touch hers, Mamie put the pan back on the stove and stirred the hot chocolate for her, pushing it toward her.

"Drink it. It will do you good."

Mamie was astounding, Teddi thought. Imagine, talking this way after what Dora had done! As if she still cared about this young woman who had tried to cheat her.

There was pain in Mamie's face, yes. Teddi could see it. But not the kind of complete disheartenment she had imagined. "How long have you known she wasn't really Ricky's wife?" she demanded abruptly.

143

"Oh, dear. I was a little bit suspicious at the beginning, until I saw that marriage certificate. I haven't seen anyone's proof of marriage for years. I didn't know what it was supposed to look like. Where did you get it?"

Dora was visibly shrinking in her chair. "Roger made it. On his brother's computer."

"I guess I was still a bit uncertain," Mamie said. "Which is, I suppose, why I never even called Ned about her, not even after the baby came." She'd brought a bag of marshmallows to the table and dropped them into each of the cups, then slumped into her own chair. "There were so many things. She was nearly ready to give birth to a child, yet Ricky hadn't written to me about a marriage. He never did write much, but surely he would have called me? That really bothered me, but it was possible, I supposed. A lot of men don't stay in touch with their families, even when there's been no estrangement. They mean to, but they just don't get around to doing it. Look how seldom we hear from Ned. The trouble was, too, that I wanted so badly to believe this was Ricky's child. I let myself overlook some of the indications that there was little proof."

"I told Roger it wouldn't work." Dora sounded sullen now, again near tears. "There would be too many things I wouldn't know. He said I'd be able to get *you* to talk enough to find them out. He said once the baby was born, we'd be able to twist you around our little fingers. You'd be besotted with him. I never heard that word before, but that's what he said. Besotted."

"And what was supposed to happen then?" Mamie

asked, sipping at her cocoa. "When I became besotted with the baby? Were you going to stay here indefinitely? Let me help raise him and support both of you?"

"We were going to figure out a way to get the insurance money. I'm not sure how, but Roger's smart. He'd have worked out something."

"Forge a will leaving everything to my grandson?" Mamie asked with a wry twist of her mouth. "Maybe even arrange an accident for me, to make sure you didn't have to wait too long to inherit?"

Alarm brought Dora's head up. "No! We'd never have done anything like that!"

Wouldn't they? Teddi wondered. She didn't like Roger much. She suspected that he would have been capable of almost any action to get what he wanted. A moment later Dora confirmed this.

"I wasn't supposed to have to stay here very long," Dora said. "I told him I couldn't, and he said I wouldn't have to. He didn't like the job at the airport, and he said if we had the insurance money he could quit and we'd go somewhere else. I hoped he'd decide it would be okay to keep the baby with us if there was enough money—"

Mamie's voice cut sharply through her words. "Did you consider *not* having the baby?"

"*I* didn't. Roger was annoyed when I told him I was pregnant. He said babies are expensive, and messy, and fussy. First he suggested I get rid of it, before it was born, but I refused to do that. He still didn't want it, so when he came up with this idea, I let him talk me into it. I thought this would solve everything until I got up here, and the baby was born, and then he started talking about . . ."

She broke off, her eyes filling once more with tears.

Mamie was gentle now. "What did he talk about, Dora? That you couldn't bear to think of?"

"He said you'd maybe want to take Danny and raise him. So we wouldn't have to. He said if we couldn't get the insurance money any other way, you'd probably hand it over in order to keep him. If you thought he was your grandchild, I mean."

"And how did you feel about giving away your child?"

Dora didn't seem to notice anything odd about Mamie's voice, but Teddi did. There was an icy edge to it that Teddi had never heard before.

"I told him I wouldn't do it. I refused to talk about giving the baby away. I hung up on him the last time, and then he came up here to talk to me in person. He thinks he can sweet-talk me into anything."

"And can he?" It was still there, velvet over a hint of ice, or steel. Maybe steel, Teddi thought.

Dora was suddenly ferocious. "Not this time. I'm not giving away my baby."

In the ensuing silence, Teddi sipped at her hot chocolate, glad it was almost hot enough to burn. Dora had been found out. There wasn't much she could do, now, was there? No matter what the unknown Roger wanted.

Mamie finally spoke. "How do you feel about being married to a man who doesn't want you to keep your child?"

"Right this minute," Dora said with a spark of anger, "I'd like to strangle him."

"But you can't do that. So what *will* you do?" Mamie asked.

For a moment Dora looked confused, as if she'd forgotten that the original plan was now in a shambles. Then, as full comprehension swept over her, she muttered, "I don't know."

"Do you want to be married to a man who refuses to let you keep your baby? Or risk staying with him when he resents the child and might abuse it?"

Obviously the idea had not occurred to Dora. Color flooded her pale face. "I'd never let anybody hurt Danny!"

A knock on the back door made their heads turn in that direction to see Jason's face through the window. Teddi got up to let him in.

He stepped into the kitchen, uncertain at seeing them all sitting companionably, as it must have seemed, around the table.

"Uh . . . maybe we'd better talk outside," he told Teddi.

She stared at the red welt across his forehead. "What happened to you? Did . . . did Roger attack you?"

"Roger? Is that his name? The guy I was chasing?"

Dora stood up, nearly spilling her cocoa. "You were chasing Roger?"

Mamie rose, too. "What's going on? Is Roger *here*?"

"He came to demand that I go out and talk to him, later. After you were all asleep. About . . . what we were going to do next." Dora was still flushed, from embarrassment this time. It was clearly difficult for her to adjust to the realization that none of the things she and Roger had planned were going to happen. "Why were you chasing him?"

"Did he hurt you?" Teddi demanded, still held by the red welt.

"No, he never even saw me. He had a car parked around the corner. I got the license number, for what that's worth. It's an old Camaro. California plates." His gaze settled on Dora. "I think the rest of you know something I don't."

"I'll explain it in a minute," Teddi assured him. "What happened to your forehead?"

"That's why I was late getting here after you whistled. My little sister left a skate on the stairs and I didn't bother turning on the hall light because I was in a hurry. I stepped on the skate and fell." He touched the raised weal. "I think this was from the edge of the railing. Who's Roger?"

"My husband," Dora said almost inaudibly.

"So Danny's *not* Ricky's kid at all." Jason's gaze swept from one of them to the other.

"No," Teddi said. Dora looked so woebegone, she almost felt sorry for her.

Apparently Mamie felt some pity for her, too. "It was a terrible thing to do," she said without rancor, which Teddi thought was pretty big of her.

Dora nodded. Twin tears slid down her cheeks, which were back to their normal pallid state. She raised her palms to wipe them off.

"You made so many mistakes," Mamie went on. "You

didn't know much about my son, and what you did express was wrong. Did you just expect me to accept you as Ricky's widow with so little proof? Only a faked marriage license, no picture of him, and that insurance policy? I wanted Danny enough so that I almost decided to take him on whatever terms I could get him, even if you were a fraud."

Teddi wanted to reach out and hug her, as Mamie would have done had their situations been reversed, but she felt frozen into immobility.

"I called the number he'd given for a home phone," Mamie continued, "and got his landlady. He was living in a rooming house, and she didn't know anything about a wife. She knew he'd been killed in that plane crash, and she didn't know where to send his belongings. I asked her to ship them to me here. How could you possibly have thought you would get away with it, Dora?"

More tears followed the first ones. After a moment, Mamie dug into a pocket for a handkerchief and passed it over.

Dora mopped ineffectually at her face and blew her nose. "What are you going to do? Are you going to have us arrested?"

"I think we need some help in dealing with Roger, at least. Where's he staying?"

Dora shrugged. "Just in his car, I think. He probably doesn't have the money for a motel."

"Why did you risk stealing money from me, when getting caught would have blown your whole scheme? Did you think I wouldn't miss a twenty-dollar bill, nor notice when it was put back?"

"I put it back," Dora said defensively. "I didn't really steal it."

"But why did you take it in the first place?"

"I needed to talk to Roger. I had to call him. There were too many things I didn't know what to do about. I thought *she*"—and here she looked at Teddi—"was looking at me suspiciously and I didn't know what to do. I knew it would cost more to call than I had in coins; I had to have enough for a long conversation, and I didn't dare call from the house. It would have showed up on your phone bill."

"So how were you able to put the money back?" Teddi asked.

"I tried to get change for the twenty at the gas station, but the attendant said his money was all locked up at night. So he told me I could make a collect call without having to have any cash. I didn't break the twenty."

"When are you supposed to meet Roger?" Mamie asked. "And where?"

Dora gulped pathetically. At least it would have seemed pathetic if she hadn't tried to do such a rotten thing to Mamie. "Midnight. He said he'd be parked around the corner again."

Mamie looked past Dora to Teddi and Jason. "I think it's time to call my lawyer. It's kind of late, but Joe's a friend from church. I think he'll advise me even at this time of night. This needs to be reported to the police, Dora. You can't attempt fraud and extortion this way and expect not to have to face the consequences."

Dora's face crumpled, and she slid back into her chair

and leaned forward over the table, sobbing softly.

In the adjoining room, Danny began to wail.

"I'll get him," Teddi offered, and hurried to scoop the infant out of his basket.

"Poor little toad," she whispered into his soft hair. "What's going to become of you?"

It was a problem for which there seemed to be no immediate solution. The baby was taken to his mother to be fed. Dora took him back to her room, tears soaking her shirt front, while Mamie talked on the phone.

Jason was looking at his watch as she hung up and announced that both the lawyer and the police would be at the corner at the appropriate time.

"My folks will be wondering what's going on. I'd better check in with them. But if it's okay with you, Mrs. Thrane, I'd kind of like to stick around and see what happens."

Mamie nodded, then, when Jason was gone, addressed Teddi. "You knew the money had been taken out of the jar, too, didn't you? Yet you didn't tell me about it."

"I was afraid you'd think that I'd taken it," Teddi admitted, flushing.

Mamie gave her a hug. "No, no, dear, I never thought that for a minute. If we'd shared our suspicions, I guess we'd have brought this to a conclusion a lot sooner."

"I knew you *wanted* Danny to be your grandson," Teddi said. "I thought it would hurt you terribly to realize he wasn't."

Mamie released her. "Oh, I did want him to be Ricky's child. But there were so many things that didn't fit. I guess right from the beginning, before he was even born, I doubted Dora's story. But I felt sorry for her. She *was* going to have a baby, and she appeared to be all alone and desperate for help and a place to stay. God forgive me, but there were moments when I seriously considered letting her get away with it, and pretending Danny really was mine, too."

"What'll happen to Danny if his parents go to jail?" Teddi asked in a small voice.

"I don't know. He'll need to be cared for, one way or another. I don't know if they'd let me take him or not. I'll have to ask Joe about that."

Teddi stared at her in wonder. "You'd keep him? Even knowing what's happened?"

"It's not his fault. I *do* love him, you know. The same as I'd love any child who needed me, and I think Danny does right now. For a while, at least. Teddi, I have a splitting headache. Would you massage my temples the way you do, see if we can make it back off?"

When Jason came back, he and Teddi and Mamie sat around the kitchen table, waiting for whatever would happen with the lawyer and the police. Dora sat by herself in the rocker in her room, holding the baby, unable to stop weeping.

When Mamie's friend Joe finally stopped by the house, it was nearly two A.M.

"He was there, in his car, right where he said he'd be. Offered no resistance. Do you want them to take the girl in tonight, too?"

"I don't think she's a flight risk," Mamie decided.

"Leave her here until morning. Then we'll go down to police headquarters together, if that's all right? I'd like to have you there, too, Joe. What about the baby, if both its parents are in jail? Can you do anything to arrange for us to keep him here? She's nursing him, but I wouldn't think she'd want to take him to jail with her. We'd have to get bottles and formula, that kind of thing, before Dora and Danny are separated."

"I'll see what I can do," Joe said gruffly.

When he had gone, Jason stood up and stretched. "Well, I'd better head for home before my dad calls the cops after *me*. I guess tomorrow's going to be pretty busy. You think we'd better postpone the tennis lesson?"

"Yeah," Teddi agreed. She couldn't even think about tennis until this matter was settled.

"But I'll talk to you in the afternoon, okay? When you know what else is going to happen."

"I'm counting on it," Teddi told him, smiling for what seemed to be the first time in a long while.

She walked with him to the back door.

"Boy," Jason said on his way out, "wait'll I tell my cousin Jenny what came of those things I wanted her to investigate. Even if Mamie had already called his landlady."

She'd have to tell Callie all the details, too, Teddi thought. But for tonight, she thought she was going to go upstairs and offer a prayer of thanks that she was still here, and Mamie was okay, and even Danny would probably be all right.

"Good night," she told Jason quietly as she closed the door behind him and locked it.

Mamie was standing there, waiting, when she turned. Without words, they went into each other's arms. They stood that way for what seemed a long time, tears running down both their faces, until finally Mamie drew back and reached for the box of tissues on the counter.

"I suppose we ought to get some sleep," Mamie said. "Tomorrow's going to be a very long day."

"I don't know if I *can* sleep," Teddi said uncertainly. "Mamie, could we just sit and talk a little longer?"

"How about if we lie on my bed, with just a night-light on, until we get sleepy?" Mamie suggested.

And so they did, and before Teddi drifted off she heard Dora in the room across the hall, making small sounds as she put Danny back in the bassinet.

Teddi's emotions were in such turmoil, she couldn't sort them out. Not tonight. But Mamie would be there tomorrow, and Mamie would make it all come out as right as it could, for Dora and Danny and herself.

And for me, Teddi thought. *And for me*.

And she slept without dreaming and without fear.